A Child Shall
Lead Them

A Child Shall Lead Them

G. D. Ballein

To order additional copies of this book, contact:
Xlibris Corporation
1-888-795-4274
www.Xlibris.com
Orders@Xlibris.com
27360

Preface

This book would not have been possible without the encouragement, patience and support of my wife, Lorna. I am grateful for those who offered observations, suggestions and corrections. Lorna and Judy Plice read numerous rewrites. My daughter, Deirdre, Nancy Townsell, Geneva Peterson and Sharon Mikkelson were also very helpful.

Prologue

From the safety of their walls the people of Jerusalem watched the Roman army surround the city. Yellow plumed helmets and red capes of thousands of Roman soldiers stood out clearly against the brown hills, the hot sun glistening off their spears. The city was in turmoil, and the people were terrified. When the defenders refused to bargain, Pompey ordered siege weapons from Tyre on the Mediterranean seacoast. The Roman soldiers fanned out over the hills to cut down trees to build timber and earthen ramps for a two-pronged attack. One would be against the northern wall, the other against the western wall. As work on the ramps progressed, catapults and battering ramps inched forward.

Finally, the battering rams were in position to hammer at the great limestone walls. For over three months the Jews fought fiercely, almost bringing the siege to a halt. But the walls were breached in 63 B.C. Three Roman legions, comprised of 6,000-8,000 men each, poured through the opening. Thousands of Jewish defenders fell under the invaders' swords. Many others hurled themselves to their deaths off the walls rather than surrender. In all, over 12,000

Jews were killed. Then Pompey and his men entered the Jew's most sacred inner chamber of the Temple, the *Holy of Holies*. It was a place where only the Jewish High Priest was permitted to go. Surprisingly, the Romans didn't disturb either the Temple treasury or the Temple itself.

Later, Rome divided the Jewish kingdom into two provinces; *Judea* in the south, *Galilee* in the north. Another province, *Samaria*, lay in the middle. They became pawns in the growing struggle for power in the very heart of Rome itself between Pompey, Crassus and Julius Caesar. Three years after Pompey defeated the defenders of Jerusalem, the three ambitious men formed an uneasy alliance known as the *First Triumvirate*.

For centuries Rome ruled Palestine via puppet kings and Roman governors. Rome was the indisputable power of the known world. Jewish patriots, who continued to fight for freedom, were called *Zealots*. There were many revolts, but Rome always won in the end. Nothing could outlast Rome's mighty empire. And yet . . .

Chapter One

Thirty years after the birth of Jesus Christ, thirteen-year-old Gideon fished on the *Sea of Galilee* with his father, Elhanan, and older brother, Harim. It was a hot, clear, windless summer day with low humidity. They pulled hard on their net filled with fish. Their lips parched, their hands chapped, naked except for loincloths around their waists. Their sleek, olive-colored skin glistened with sweat. The smell of the sea was strong as seagulls circled above the boat waiting to swoop down to gather up any fish they could.

Harim tugged on the net. "Caesar should be thrilled so many of our people are catching so much fish today," he said. "It will make Tiberius richer from the taxes he robs from us."

Harim had just turned seventeen. He loved and respected his father, Elhanan, in every way save one. He felt his father was too accommodating towards their Roman rulers. Gideon sighed but didn't say anything. He disliked Harim's disrespectful attitude toward their father's lack of hatred for Rome. He looked at his father, wishing his older brother would keep his mouth shut.

Elhanan loathed the prospect of getting into another heated argument with Harim but wasn't about to allow his son to go unrebuked. He stopped pulling on his end of the net. "Listen, Harim, we're fishing for our family, not Rome," he said, glaring at Harim. "Yes, we'll pay taxes to Rome but you and your self-appointed revolutionaries will not stop it." He resumed pulling the net. "Our history is written in the blood of young men who tried to rebel against them. I've seen too many men hanging on crosses."

Harim glanced at his father but dropped the volatile subject, much to Gideon's relief. "How many fish do you think we caught today, Father?" Gideon asked.

Elhanan smiled at Gideon. *You're wise for one so young, Gideon,* he thought. "I'd guess between eighty and a hundred fish so far. A very good catch indeed but we still have at least an hour longer to try for more."

They had some additional success, but didn't catch nearly as many fish as they had earlier. Elhanan straightened up to stretch his tired back. "The sun will be setting soon so we better head for shore," he said. "It's been a good day. Set the sail, Harim."

The three exhausted fishermen made their way to shore. When they got there they pulled their boat on the beach and unloaded their catch onto a cart. Upon arriving home they salted the fish and finally walked into their modest house in Capernaum.

Elhanan's home of stone and mud bricks was typical of Jewish houses. Inside the entrance was an open courtyard that served as an open-air kitchen. Flanking the courtyard were two rooms with cobblestone floors. One side room was for the family's domestic animals. The other was a smaller all—purpose room. Across the back of the house stretched a long, narrow communal room. Timber beams supported a second floor, reached by a ladder, containing the bedrooms. Another ladder led up from the second floor to a flat roof used to store large jars of grain and oil.

Elhanan's wife, Sarah, and their youngest son, Jehoram, greeted them with broad smiles. Sarah had married Elhanan when she was fifteen. She had smooth, olive skin and long, wavy black hair. She, like all Jews of both sexes, wore a white linen tunic covering the body from the lower neck to well below the knees. Over this was draped a light blue cloak made of wool. A red cloth tied around her waist kept the voluminous cloak from blowing in the wind and getting in the way of movement.

Elhanan kissed Sarah on the cheek as Harim and Gideon joined Jehoram around the table. Elhanan, expecting his daughter would be home, sat down at the table. "Where's Rachel?" he asked.

Sarah poured some ruby-red wine and handed it to Elhanan. "She went to see how Martha is doing with her new baby, Joshua," she answered. She sat down at the opposite end of the table from Elhanan next to an empty chair meant for Rachel. "You know Rachel. She'll insist on helping anyway she can."

"She better be home soon or I'll send Harim to fetch her," Elhanan said. "It's getting too late for her to be out by herself."

No sooner did Elhanan get the words out than Rachel entered the house. She kissed both parents on the cheek, turned and looked at the table. Dates, cheese, fresh warm bread, honey and roasted lamb were already on the table. Rachel's face turned red for being late.

Rachel resembled her mother who looked young enough to be her older sister. Similar to her mother in weight and height, it was difficult to distinguish between them from behind. Rachel, at twenty, was the eldest child and only daughter. She had been betrothed but her prospective husband died of an illness four months before they were to be married. Her parents hadn't pledged her to anyone else since his death, and it bothered Rachel that she still wasn't married.

"I'm sorry I'm late," Rachel said. "I was so busy helping Martha that I didn't notice the sun was setting."

"How are Martha and the baby?" Sarah asked.

"The baby seems to be doing fine, but Martha is still very weak," Rachel answered, sighing. "She's worried she might not be strong enough to go with her husband when the baby is circumcised. Her husband can't help her with their other son because he has to fish whenever the weather allows it."

"You don't have to tell me," Sarah replied, grinning. "You'd like to go there as long as Martha needs help." Elhanan didn't say anything. This was his wife's decision and he respected their custom and religious teaching about helping their neighbors. "You can go there after you finish your duties here for as long as Martha needs you," Sarah said.

Neither Rachel nor Elhanan were surprised by Sarah's compliance. It was as unimaginable for Sarah to have *refused* Rachel's desire to be helpful as it would have been for Rachel not to want to do it.

Elhanan reached out, took Jehoram's hand in his left hand and Gideon's in his right. Then the others all held hands in anticipation of the blessing. Elhanan lifted his eyes toward heaven. "Blessed art Thou, O Lord, King of the universe, who provides us with food from the earth."

They opened their eyes after Elhanan's prayer and helped themselves to the food. "How was fishing today, Father?" Jehoram asked.

"Very good, thanks to the tremendous help by Harim and Gideon," Elhanan answered with a proud expression. "They're born to be successful fishermen, those two."

The entire family realized Jehoram would *never* be a fisherman. Born lame, he managed to get along quite well on his wooden crutch his father had made for him. He was tall for a seven-year-old and on the skinny side. His condition wasn't something that caused any of them to feel embarrassed for talking openly about it. They treated him just like everyone else.

Meal times were sacred occasions for Jewish families and were not rushed into. They enjoyed them for the fellowship it provided as much as for the food. But on this occasion Harim hardly said a word. Sarah, noticing his sullen demeanor, let it pass without asking Harim what was bothering him. She assumed Harim and Elhanan had another argument.

Following their meal Elhanan picked up Jehoram the way he did every evening. He squeezed him affectionately as he carried him to bed. Elhanan sat on the edge of Jehoram's bed as he asked, "What did you do today, Jehoram?"

Jehoram always seemed happy. "I started carving a fishing boat from a piece of wood I found," Jehoram answered, beaming proudly. "I want it to look just like the one you have. Rachel gave me a linen rag for the sail."

"I'd like to see it when you're done," Elhanan said. He stood up and smiled at Jehoram. "Try to go to sleep now, Jehoram." He rubbed Jehoram on the top of his head and bent over to kiss him. "I'll see you in the morning. I love you."

Elhanan went down the narrow steps to join the others. Rachel was washing the clay dishes in a bowl of water, Sarah was sewing a torn sheet, and Harim and Gideon were playing a game with wood sticks. Elhanan poured a cup of wine and looked out the window. It was a warm evening with a full moon. He heard a wolf howl in the distance.

Elhanan turned around and drained his cup of wine. "It's a nice evening tonight," he said, smiling at Sarah. "I'm going to go for a short walk. Anyone want to join me?"

Sarah put down her sewing. "I will, as long as we don't go too far," she answered, standing up. "I don't know about you but I'm getting sleepy."

"I'll go with you, too," Rachel said.

The three of them strolled fifty or sixty yards, stopping to admire the moon reflecting off the Sea of Galilee. The rolling hills on the other side of the sea were silhouetted against the dark, blue sky. They looked at the lights from oil lamps coming through the windows of many of the houses.

"God chose a magnificent place to lead His people to under Moses centuries ago," Elhanan said, sighing. "I only wish He would send the Messiah to free us from Rome's oppression. The slaves waited four hundred years before He delivered them from Egypt. God help us if we have to wait that long to be free from Rome." He sounded sad, but not without hope.

"God's timing isn't our timing, Elhanan," Sarah said, sliding her hand into his. "God always keeps His promises if we remain faithful." They walked a little farther before turning home.

Later, as Elhanan and Sarah snuggled in bed, she sensed he was troubled about something. She took a deep breath and slowly let it out. "Did you have another argument with Harim?" she asked in a whisper.

Elhanan pulled her to his chest. "It wasn't an argument, but I'm afraid he's becoming more brazen with his criticism of Rome. He never goes so far as to be disrespectful, but he's headed for great danger if he keeps on complaining about the Romans. All he needs to do is lose his temper someday and say something in front of a person who wants to ingratiate himself with the Romans. If he does that he will be arrested for treason."

Sarah sat up and rested on her elbow. She looked at Elhanan, her heart pounding in alarm. "You don't really think he would be that foolish, do you?"

He pulled her to his chest. "I hope not, Sarah, but Rome doesn't require much to throw innocent people in the dungeon. Just a passing comment about taxes is enough. I have warned him again and again about his constant criticism, but he only sees it as weakness on my part. I also told him to stop hanging around some of his friends who are sympathizers with the Zealots. That's what concerns me the most. Even if Harim is wise enough to keep his mouth shut he might be arrested just for associating with them. I know there are many Jews who secretly agree with the Zealots' desire for freedom, but are afraid the Zealots might make things worse."

"Do you think Harim has been talking with a Zealot?"

"I'm not sure. I don't know of anyone in particular but I think that he has."

"Why do you think that?" Sarah asked.

"Harim's mentioned a man called Zedekiah several times, and from what I've heard Zedekiah is a Zealot. I don't know if Harim has talked with him or only knows about him."

"Do you think Harim understands how dangerous it is to associate with the Zealots?" Sarah asked. "Most of our friends think the Zealots cause more problems than they solve."

"They have good reason to feel that way. When the Zealots rebelled in the past it always ended up with the Romans slaughtering innocent people. The Romans aren't particular whom they kill when they suspect rebellion is afoot. I just wish Harim would understand that. Whenever I try to warn him he thinks I'm a coward."

"I don't understand how Harim can feel that way about you, of all people. You always taught him to respect us. Do you really think he would disobey you if you *demanded* him to stay away from them?"

"Naturally he would never disobey me when we're together, but he isn't with me all the time. He's a man of seventeen now. Even Rabbi Jacobs says Harim is a man and must be treated like one. There's little I can do or say besides offer him my advice. And like I said, he feels my advice is a sign of cowardice."

*　　*　　*

Everyone was awake early the next morning. They ate a hearty breakfast of dried figs cooked in molasses, fresh goats milk and bread made of barley. After they finished eating they tended to their assorted chores. Harim and Gideon made minor repairs to their nets, Elhanan checked the sail on their fishing boat and Rachel helped her mother around the house.

Sarah smiled at Rachel. "You can go help Martha now."

"Thank you," Rachel replied, heading for the open door. "I won't be late this time."

Martha lived five hundred yards from Rachel's home and Rachel hurried to get there to help take care of Martha's two young sons. The streets were alive with activities. Merchants brought out their wares to arrange them on tables in front of their shops. Weavers displayed their colored materials, cobblers their sandals, wine merchants their jars of wine and the perfume mixers their sweet-smelling ointments and perfumes.

Rachel's thoughts were on Martha and her baby as she rushed passed the noisy crowd along the dusty street. She hadn't gone very far when she noticed three Roman soldiers walking from the direction she was headed. They wore ankle-high leather sandals, and on the upper torso, a breastplate of segmented metal designed to allow the arms and shoulders freedom of movement. Their heads were covered with an iron helmet, and underneath their breastplate, a bright red shirt that went halfway down their thighs. They didn't carry their shields or spears, but had a sword in a heavy leather sheath hanging from the waist.

Rachel covered her face with her white linen scarf, lowering her head in hopes they would ignore her as had happened before. This time was an exception. She was almost passed them when one soldier suddenly grabbed her by the arm.

"We're looking for a Zealot by the name of Zedekiah," he said, glaring at her with cruel eyes. "He supposedly lives around here. Do you know where we can find him?" He was short, heavyset and had a deep scar that went the length of his left cheek.

Rachel was terrified as he squeezed her arm. "No sir, I don't know anyone by that name," she answered, trying to sound calm.

His yellow teeth showed when he grinned with a wicked expression. "Well, I think you're lying. I think we better take you to see our captain. Maybe then you'll feel more like talking."

Rachel felt him squeeze her arm even tighter. Her heart pounded rapidly in her chest, gasping for breath from fear. "Honestly, sir, I've never heard of him."

He enjoyed twisting her arm behind her back, causing her to wince from the pain. "All you Jews are liars," he said, laughing and glancing at his comrades. "You better come with us."

Another soldier slapped his comrade on the bare arm with the flat end of his sword. "Let her go, you brute," he said, "or I'll use the sharp side of my blade on your neck. She obviously doesn't know anything about Zedekiah."

Rachel was astonished and relieved by his action. He was of a higher rank than the soldier threatening Rachel, although she knew nothing of their rank. He was tall, and muscular with firm limbs. He stood erect and square as if he were cut from a giant cedar. He had a straight nose and square jaw that bore witness to his manliness.

Strange, but he doesn't look Roman, Rachel thought.

When the soldier released her arm she hurried down the road toward Martha's house, still shaking from her terrifying ordeal. Martha sensed something was wrong as Rachel entered the house. She reached out, took Rachel's arm and led her to a chair. "Rachel, what on earth has happened to you?" she asked in alarm. "You're trembling all over."

Rachel collapsed on a chair, trying to breath normally. Martha sat down next to her with a worried expression. Rachel began to cry, lowering her head in her hands. When she leaned back she answered, "I was stopped by three soldiers on my way here. One of them grabbed me by the arm and insisted I tell them about some Zealot by the name of Zedekiah. When I told them I didn't know him, the one who held my arm said I lied and threatened to take me to see their captain. I was certain they were going to arrest me and throw me into prison."

Martha, flabbergasted, reached out to take Rachel by the hand. "So how did you manage to get away?"

Rachel took a deep breath. "Another soldier with kind eyes pulled out his sword and slapped the man who was holding me. He ordered him to let me go. When he did I ran here as fast as I could."

Martha, releasing Rachel's hand, leaned back with a thankful expression. "Surely God was with you, Rachel. No wonder you're shaking like a fig leaf in a windstorm." Martha smiled. "Kind eyes, you say. That's an odd description for a Roman soldier."

Rachel's face turned red, wondering why she not only had noticed his eyes but also used it to refer to him. "Thank God that's over and done with," Rachel said, sighing. "Tell me, how are you and Joshua feeling this morning?"

"Joshua is improving but I'm afraid that I'm still very weak. I can't tell you how much I appreciate your willingness to come and help out, Rachel. So does my husband."

"No more than I appreciate the chance to be with you and your boys. Besides, that's what friends are for." Rachel slapped her knees and stood up. "That's enough talk. Let's get to work. What do you want me to do first?"

Martha laughed. "Slave driver! We need some more water from the well. After you fetch some water you can take the clothes down to the stream to wash them. Then you can watch the children while I churn the butter."

Rachel grabbed a bucket and made her way to the well. One of her friends, filling her own bucket with water, greeted her. "Good morning, Rachel." Rachel seemed distracted and didn't respond. "Rachel, are you all right?"

Rachel looked at her with a blank expression for a few seconds. "Oh, good morning, Lydia. My mind was on something else. Yes, I'm fine." Rachel's mind was on her Roman rescuer. "How are you?"

"I'm fine, too." Lydia thought about asking Rachel what was on her mind but decided not to pry.

*　　*　　*

On their way back from fishing Elhanan, Harim and Gideon saw something that made their hearts sink. A detachment of soldiers marched through the street with a dozen or more prisoners chained together. Five of the prisoners' backs bled from having been scourged. They all looked half dead from exhaustion and their eyes were hollow. It was a horrific sight. Elhanan and his sons knew these men were on their way to die. It was obvious the prisoners knew it, too.

Elhanan glanced at Harim, but Harim's eyes were transfixed on the prisoners. Elhanan knew what his son was feeling. Compassion yes, but mostly hatred. The Jewish eyewitnesses along the street stood helpless, watching the wretched parade pass by.

After the soldiers and prisoners were gone Harim turned and glared at his father. Neither one spoke. It wasn't necessary. They knew what the other one was thinking. So did Gideon. When they arrived home Harim stayed outside as Elhanan and Gideon went inside.

"How was fishing today?" Jehoram asked.

Elhanan poured a cup of wine, sat down next to Jehoram, and gulped down his wine. "Not as good as yesterday, I'm sorry to say, Jehoram," he answered, staring at the empty cup.

Sarah and Rachel could tell from Elhanan's tone of voice and the expressions on his and Gideon's faces that something had happened. Sarah sat down next to Elhanan, reached out and put her hand on top of his. Rachel sat down opposite her father. Neither one said anything. They looked at Elhanan, waiting to see if he would say anything.

Elhanan looked at Sarah, shaking his head in despair. "On the way home we saw some prisoners being taken to the garrison by a company of soldiers." He didn't have to say more.

"Oh, my God, no," Sarah murmured under her breath. She leaned forward and whispered, "Did Harim say anything?"

"He didn't need to. We knew what each other was thinking."

* * *

Later than night Rachel lay in bed with her eyes wide open. She couldn't dismiss from her mind how she had identified the one with the kind eyes. She felt guilty for not thanking him for rescuing her from her horrible ordeal, but told herself she didn't have much of a chance of thanking him. She realized it was unlikely she would have the opportunity in the future. One thing she knew for certain was she dared not tell her family anything about it. That was especially true concerning her brother, Harim. He hated the Roman soldiers enough without knowing his sister had been threatened by one of them.

Chapter Two

The weather the following day made it impossible to go fishing. It wasn't raining but the powerful winds were always the prelude to a violent storm on the Sea of Galilee. Even if it didn't rain the wind churned the water enough to sink a fishing boat.

After everyone had eaten breakfast Elhanan said, "As long as it isn't raining I'm going to check our roof for leaks. When you three are done with your chores you can do whatever you want as long as you're back before it rains."

Rachel picked olives and boiled them in brine, Harim chopped wood for the brick oven in front of the house and Gideon scrubbed the cart used to carry their fish with lye. When they finished Rachel went to help Martha, Gideon went to see what his friends were doing and Harim said he wanted to go for a walk. Jehoram had no choice but to stay at home as he did every day of his life.

When Rachel arrived at Martha's home she knocked on the open door. Martha's husband, Caleb, standing behind the door, peeked around to see who was there. Caleb, a fisherman like Rachel's father and brothers, was home due to the approaching storm. Rachel realized she wouldn't be needed.

"Good morning, Rachel," Caleb said with a broad smile. "Come on in. You look surprised to see me here today."

"I admit that I am, but I ought to have realized you would be home," Rachel replied as she walked into the house, blushing.

Caleb, noticing her embarrassed expression, said, "As long as you're here, Rachel, I'd appreciate it if you would stay for a while so I can go check my fishing nets."

That was a considerate gesture on Caleb's part, Rachel thought. *Still, he doesn't have any sons old enough to help him the way my father does. He probably can use the chance to do what needs to be done.* She returned the smile. "I'll be glad to stay here while you're gone."

"I appreciate that very much," he replied. "Thank you."

Martha sat at the table nursing the baby as Caleb kissed her and left. "Thanks for coming over, Rachel," Martha said. "I know you might be thinking Caleb was just being polite but he really does need to repair his net."

""I realized that, but even if he didn't it's like Caleb to be thoughtful."

Martha looked at her baby. "Caleb and I are afraid I'm might not be well enough to go for purification on time," she said with a deep sigh. "Caleb intends to talk with Rabbi Jacobs about it." Her oldest son ran up to Rachel as Martha asked, "How's everything at your place?"

"Strained, to tell the truth," Rachel answered, picking up three-year-old Joshua and hugging him. "My father and brothers saw some prisoners being led through the street yesterday on their way home from fishing. Harim didn't say one word last night." She put Joshua down and sat next to Martha. "The only thing he said this morning at breakfast was that he was going for a walk. He even said that with a great deal of bitterness in his voice."

"I'm very sorry to hear that." Martha handed the baby to Rachel, who smothered the baby in kisses. "I don't understand why Harim takes out his anger on your father because of what the Romans do. I'm afraid Harim is too young to realize the harm he's causing. Few things are more painful than family arguments."

It still wasn't raining an hour later when Caleb came home from tending to the repair work on his nets. Rachel and Martha had enjoyed their time together, but it was time for Rachel to leave. She kissed Joshua and his baby brother.

"Thanks for helping Martha while I was gone, Rachel," Caleb said. "Your staying here was a big help to me as well."

"It was my pleasure, Caleb."

Rachel said goodbye and left for home. Rachel hadn't walked very far when she noticed two soldiers in the distance going into a shoemaker's shop. Just the sight of them caused her to shiver, recalling her previous encounter. Then Rachel thought, *I wonder if one of them might have been the one with the kind eyes.* Rachel's face turn red in self-rebuke. *Easy there, Rachel, one act of consideration doesn't mean he is anything more than a ruthless soldier.*

Nevertheless, she walked slower just in case they came out of the shoemaker's shop and she could get a better look at them. They did, but they walked in the opposite direction. She never saw their faces. She stood to watch them for a minute in disappointment. She felt sad as she continued walking home, her mind unable to free itself from the thought of her unknown liberator.

Meanwhile, Gideon went to Joash's house to see what he was doing. "I'm sorry, Gideon, you just missed him," Joash's mother said. "He just left with Daddeus to go over to Elizabad's house."

Gideon took off after them. When he got there the four friends had more energy than ideas as to what to do. Lacking more thrilling prospects, they decided to go watch Elizabad's uncle at work making bricks. It didn't take long for them to grow bored and head back to Elizabad's home.

On the way they were surprised to find the road blocked by a large crowd. The crowd appeared to be excited and attentive at the same time. "They're following that man up front," Daddeus said. "I wonder who he is?"

"I don't know," Elizabad replied. "We don't have anything else to do. Why don't we follow them?"

They joined the procession. Most of the people in crowd were ordinary folk, but there were a number of religious leaders and influential elders as well. The four youngsters wanted to hear what the leader of the procession was saying but from their position near the rear of the parade only were able to hear bits and pieces.

"It sounded like the leader said something about God's Kingdom," Joash said. "I wonder who he is?"

Then Gideon overheard a man in the crowd tell another man, "Jesus is the Messiah."

The other man replied in an angry tone, "And I tell you you're crazy! Jesus is the son of a carpenter in Nazareth by the name of Joseph, not the son of David."

Gideon stopped walking and grabbed Joash's arm. "I heard my father arguing with Harim about the Zealots several days ago. My father told him the *Messiah* would free us from our sins and give us peace, not Harim's friends. He said God had promised for centuries to one day send a Messiah to rule our people. I wonder if the man leading the procession is this Jesus they're arguing about? It would be fantastic if this man actually were the Messiah."

"Didn't you hear a man say Jesus isn't the Messiah?" Joash replied.

"Yes, but the other man thought Jesus *was* the Messiah," Gideon answered.

"I can't hear anything," Elizabad complained. "This is even worse than watching bricks being made. Let's find something to do that is more fun than this. I'll beat all of you to my house."

The four friends raced each other to Elizabad's house. When they got there Elizabad's father looked at the exhausted foursome. "What have you four been up to today?" he asked. His voice sounded curious, not like an accusation they did something wrong.

"We went to watch Uncle Zerah making bricks," Elizabad answered. "On the way back here we followed a crowd of people who were following some teacher."

Elizabad took his son's arm and looked him in the eyes. "Listen, Elizabad, you better not get mixed up with any crowds, understand? You're old enough to know the Romans don't like crowds one bit." He released his son's arm. "Who was this teacher, anyway?"

"I'm not sure but I did overhear one man say the name Jesus," Gideon answered in a timid voice. "I think it might have been Jesus."

Elizabad's father leaned back in his chair. "Jesus, you say. I heard about this man. Apparently he is a rabbi of some kind who has been going from place to place teaching about God. Some people have claimed he also has healed a good many people, but Rabbi Jacobs has said he's a heretic. I think you better stay away from this Jesus. That includes his followers as well."

Gideon's eyes opened wide in astonishment. *Could Jesus heal Jehoram?* he wondered. He kept his thoughts to himself, not wanting Elizabad's father to think he was interested in Jesus.

*　　*　　*

Harim's mind was on the prisoners he had seen being led to the Roman garrison. He strolled nonchalantly along the edge of a farmer's wheat field when he heard a voice from behind calling to him. He turned around and saw one of his friends running to catch up with him. Harim was glad to see Onias.

Onias' hatred for Romans surpassed even that of Harim. His father, arrested fourteen years earlier for not paying enough taxes, died in prison leaving his family destitute. Onias' mother and three older brothers were then sold into slavery. Onias would have been sold as well, but no one wanted to buy a skinny eight-year-old boy.

When Onias reached him he bent over to catch his breath. "I thought that was you, Harim," he said, gasping for breath. He stood straight up with his hands on his hips. "Did you know there was a meeting with Zedekiah in our usual spot?"

"No, I didn't! No one bothered to tell me anything about it. How did you find out?"

"That's what I thought when I saw you going in the wrong direction," Onias replied. "Anyway, Imlah told me about the meeting."

Without saying anything more they jogged back along the wheat-field several hundred yards. Then they turned and ran up a hillside another six hundred yards until they entered a large grove of trees. They walked up to a secluded spot near a boulder in the middle of the woods, used numerous times before as a meeting place. Harim and Onias staggered up to the forty or more young men. The startled men jumped to their feet in a panic.

Harim grinned and said, "Easy there. It's only Onias and me."

The men breathed a sigh of relief and sat back down on the ground. The only exception was Imlah who remained standing. He glared angrily at the two latecomers. "You two scared the daylights out of us, you idiots! Besides, you're late!"

"That's because you never bothered to tell me about the meeting, genius!" Harim snapped back.

Zedekiah raised his deep, gruff voice to put an end to the bickering. "Would you two shut-up!" He was the Zealot the soldiers had questioned Rachel about earlier. A big, powerful man in his early thirties, Zedekiah was the leader of the group. He had once witnessed the crucifixion of over a hundred Jews for insurrection.

No one said a word as Zedekiah glared at Imlah and Harim with a menacing look. Then Zedekiah resumed his speech. "Every day the Romans strangle our people, producing more and more victims. But it also causes more men to be willing to strike out for freedom. Hundreds of men acting on their own can do little but end up getting butchered. We *must* be organized if we ever expect to defeat Rome!"

Zedekiah's voice seethed with hatred for Rome, the passion and conviction in his eyes, unavoidable. "Judas Maccabee demonstrated that a century ago when he fought our enemy. Right now there are various groups forming in the hills. But they are *not* united and need more recruits. It's for patriots like us to draw more men to our cause, not fight soldiers on our own."

Athaliah, the oldest man present at thirty-eight, said, "But how can we find out if someone wants to join us without putting ourselves in danger by asking who wants to fight against Rome? We might end up talking to someone who wants to ingratiate himself to Rome by betraying us."

"The same way we found each other," Zedekiah replied. "By talking with men you *already* know, not strangers you don't know. The ones you are sure long for freedom but don't know what to do against Rome. Tell them to join us. There are thousands of men like that. Talk with them and we'll be amazed how fast we will grow into a formidable army."

Shallum rose to his feet. "Why bother waiting to get organized?" he asked, angrily. "That will only allow the Romans more time to destroy our people. I say that if one of us has the opportunity to kill a soldier he should do it then and there!"

Zedekiah understood the reason for Shallum's angry objection. Shallum's oldest son had been killed in a brief, misguided attempt to ambush a group of soldiers outside the city. Zedekiah looked at Shallum. "Don't be such a fool, Shallum. Killing one or even a dozen soldiers might give you emotional satisfaction, but that's all. What's more it will only cause the Romans to slaughter hundreds of our people in retaliation. We need to win *battles* to overthrow Rome, not kill a few soldiers now and again. We must be warriors, not assassins! Rome sends legions to conquer and control their enemies. You know how much I hate Rome. Like it or not, Shallum, we must learn from them. It will take an army to fight and win our freedom. Hatred ignites us, but it will take skill and intelligence to defeat Rome, not just passion. Our people will join us once they realize we can win but not if they think we are only committing suicide."

Harim didn't say anything but he thought Shallum *and* Zedekiah were right. *We could get organized and kill a soldier when we have the chance. Why does it have to be one or the other?*

*   *   *

After Elhanan had checked the roof he went into town to sell the fish they caught the day before. Gideon and Harim were not home when Rachel arrived home. Jehoram sat outside working on his sailboat. That meant that Rachel was in the house alone with her mother.

Rachel, sitting at the table mending a torn cloak, glanced at her mother washing vegetables. "Mother, something happened yesterday when I was going to Martha's that I want to share with you," Rachel said.

"What was that?"

"Three soldiers stopped me and asked me if I knew a man called Zedekiah." Sarah, startled, looked at Rachel.

"Don't worry, Mother, nothing happened," Rachel reassured her. "But I want to tell you *why* nothing happened. One of the soldiers threatened to take me to see their captain for questioning, but another soldier ordered him to let me go."

Sarah sighed. "Praise be to God for His mercy!"

"Ever since that happened I haven't been able to get the man who helped me out of my mind."

Sarah resumed washing the vegetables. "That's only natural, Rachel. You were frightened and he helped you."

Rachel dropped her hands in her lap. "I think it's more than just gratitude. I saw several soldiers again today and wished . . . I wished that he was one of them. I see his face all the time in my mind."

"Rachel, you probably will never see him again. And even if you did he might not recognize you or care about you. Please don't be so naïve as to assume he is as kind and considerate as that one occasion suggests. After all, he's a soldier, not a fisherman or carpenter. And most important he's a Roman—not a Jew."

Rachel was disappointed, but knew her mother was right in everything she had said. "Above all, Rachel, don't tell anyone else about any of this," Sarah cautioned. "Especially Martha and Caleb. There is no telling what our friends would do if they knew that soldiers had threatened you."

Rachel had been so upset when she told Martha what had happened she never considered Martha might tell other people about it. *I should have asked Martha to keep it a secret,* Rachel thought. *I hope Martha took it for granted it was told to her in confidence.*

Martha looked at Rachel. "Rachel, you said the soldiers were looking for Zedekiah. I wonder if that's the same man Harim has mentioned once or twice?"

Before Rachel could say anything Elhanan walked in and removed his wet cloak. He shook the water off his head, kissed Sarah on the cheek and poured a glass of wine. "I sold all our fish at the market," he announced, drinking some wine. "I see Jehoram is making good headway on his boat." He collapsed on a chair next to Rachel. "How's Martha today? I hope she's improving."

"Not much better, I'm sorry to say. Martha and Caleb are concerned she might not be able to offer herself for purification on time. She said Caleb plans on talking with Rabbi Jacobs about it."

Gideon barged into the house at that precise moment with what he thought was fantastic news. He began to speak excitedly, but his father stopped him. "Hold on there, Gideon. Dry yourself off and calm down. Then greet your mother properly before rattling off like a frightened gazelle."

Gideon blushed, walked over and kissed his mother on the cheek. Then he looked sheepishly at his father who nodded his approval. "There's a rabbi in Capernaum who can heal Jehoram!" Gideon blurted out.

The entire family was startled and stared at Gideon is disbelief. Elhanan, glad Jehoram was outside, whispered, "Not so loud, Gideon, or Jehoram will hear you." He looked at the door to see if Jehoram had heard anything. Then Elhanan laughed. "Don't tell me you believed such a ridiculous thing? Where in the world did you hear this nonsense?"

Gideon feelings were hurt. "From Elizabad's father," he answered. "He told us there was a rabbi called Jesus who has been going everywhere healing people."

"When did he tell you this?" Elhanan asked, still grinning.

"When my friends and I told him that we happened to bump into a large crowd who were following Jesus through the streets."

Elhanan, realizing Gideon's feelings were hurt, regretted he had laughed at his young son's gullibility. He motioned to Gideon to come toward him. He pulled Gideon on his lap and put his arm around his shoulder. Elhanan gazed into his sparkling eyes that seconds ago had been full of hope.

"Look, Gideon, I understand why you're so excited," Elhanan said. "We all pray that God will heal Jehoram some day. But Rabbi Jacobs has told us all about this rabbi they call Jesus. According to Rabbi Jacobs this Jesus is a false Messiah who has been deceiving people into following him by *pretending* to perform miracles, including healing people. Some of his followers have even gone so far as to claim Jesus has raised the dead. You know that's impossible. Rabbi Jacobs also said this false prophet will eventually bring all of Rome down on our people. I hate to break your heart, Gideon, but you better forget all about this troublemaker."

Gideon's tender heart *was* broken. He lowered his head and turned to walk away, stopping to look at his mother as tears came to his eyes. She smiled but it was a sad smile. Gideon trusted his father and Rabbi Jacobs. Jewish rabbis had tremendous influence over their people, especially those who followed them without doubting their word. Even the Romans granted the rabbis some authority over their communities, as long as they didn't oppose taxes or advocate rebellion. Religion and sacred teaching were of no concern for Rome and had little inclination to interfere in non-political matters. When Rabbi Jacobs, with his long, ritual fringes hanging on his clothes and leather straps bound to his forehead and arm, pointed out the finer points of religious law it wasn't open for debate. And when they pronounced another teacher a heretic or blasphemer it *had* to be true.

Consequently, Gideon's parents were astonished when Gideon did something he never did before. He looked back at his father and challenged his opinion. "But Rabbi Jacobs might be wrong about Jesus. Why should we miss the chance to ask Jesus if he *can* heal Jehoram?"

Elhanan realized Gideon wasn't trying to be defiant. Ever since Elhanan's children were young he had taught them to trust in their God who had performed mighty miracles in the past. Elhanan stared at Gideon, aware that his teaching was responsible for the inexplicable hope deep within Gideon's soul, causing him to believe Jehoram could be healed.

Elhanan sighed sadly. "You're right to believe in God's wondrous power, Gideon, but false prophets spread lies to gain supporters. Surely you realize Rabbi Jacobs knows more about such people than we do."

Before anyone could say anything more, Harim and Jehoram came into the room. Harim, dripping wet, apologized for being late and started to dry himself off. "Get out of those wet clothes, Harim, before you get sick," Sarah snapped.

Harim, relieved he didn't need to explain where he had been, went straight to his room to change clothes. Now that Jehoram was present, all discussion about Jesus ceased. Yet, Gideon still hoped his father would one day take Jehoram to see Jesus.

* * *

Rachel, having finished her chores the next morning, looked at her mother. Sarah smiled. "You don't have to ask, Rachel. You can go to Martha's now but be sure you're back before your father gets home."

"I will. May I take a loaf of bread and roll of cheese with me? I feel awkward eating their food everyday."

"Of course," Sarah answered. "Be sure to kiss the boys for me."

Rachel walked slowly out of the house. Once outside she rushed to Martha's house. When Martha opened her door she was surprised to notice Rachel panting with a flushed face. "What did you do, Rachel, run all the way here?"

Rachel took a deep breath. "As a matter of fact, I did." They went in the house, closing the door behind them. Rachel put the cheese and bread on the table as she took another deep breath. "Did you mention to anyone what I told you about the soldier who had befriended me?" Rachel asked anxiously.

"No, I didn't." Martha noticed what Rachel had placed on the table. "Thanks for the bread and cheese, but you didn't have to bring anything. I assumed you wanted it kept a secret. Why do you ask?"

Rachel sat down with a sigh. "Bless your discretion, Martha. I should have asked you to keep it to yourself. Harassing our men is one thing, but threatening women is another. My mother pointed out if our friends ever heard about it they might do something foolish."

Martha's son, Joshua, came in and crawled up on Rachel's lap. "I'm surprised that you told your mother what happened," Martha said. "Weren't you worried she might tell your father?"

"No, not really." Rachel kissed and hugged Joshua. "Thankfully, she has more sense than I do."

"So what else did your mother tell you? I doubt if she was happy to hear about the soldier with the kind eyes?"

"She was shocked when I told her that I had been stopped by the soldiers. She also pointed out I probably would never see the soldier who helped me. And even if we did see each other, he wouldn't recognize me or care about me. She was most likely right about that." She put Joshua down. "Gideon told us that he heard about a rabbi could heal Jehoram."

"Did he tell you the name of this rabbi?"

Rachel was surprised Martha wanted to know his name. "Yes, he did. He said it was Jesus. Why, did you ever hear of him?"

"Yes, I have. Caleb told me about him."

"What did he tell you?"

"He said that Jesus has made a lot of enemies among our religious leaders but also has a large following among the people. What did your parents say about Jesus?"

"Mother didn't say anything, but father told Gideon the man is a fraud who might be dangerous to our people. He also told Gideon to forget all about Jesus. Gideon was heartbroken." Rachel rose to her feet. "What can I do to help today?"

"You can take the children outside before it gets too hot. I want to try to sleep for an hour or so. The baby kept me awake most of the night."

Chapter Three

The fertile valley of *Esdraelon* lay midway between the Sea of Galilee and the Mediterranean Sea. Often called the *Jezreel Valley*, it was a plain rich in good farming land with rivers and wells. It had been an important military and commercial passageway centuries before the Romans came. It also provided easy access to maritime traffic through the valley. The olive trees were so plentiful Rabbi Jacobs once claimed it was easier to maintain an entire Roman legion of 6,000 soldiers in Galilee than to feed a single child in the barren land of Judea in the south.

Fifty Roman soldiers escorted a large caravan through the Jezreel Valley to deliver supplies from a ship that landed at the seaport of *Acco* on the Mediterranean. They were on their way to *Magdala* on the Sea of Galilee when they were ambushed. The Romans marched on a treeless plain with a rocky hill to their right. It was an ideal spot for an attack. When they were within ten miles of Magdala over two hundred Zealots attacked them from on top of the hill.

The soldiers, already exhausted from their long march in the oppressive heat, were not expecting the sudden hail of arrows and spears from the Jews hiding behind the boulders. The Romans tried to protect themselves with their shields while trying to form a protective circle. Then the overwhelming number of Zealots charged down the bank with their swords, yelling and screaming. The blazing sun behind the attackers shown directly into the soldiers' eyes made it difficult for the soldiers to see them. It was a brilliant and vicious maneuver that resulted in a complete massacre of the Romans.

The outnumbered Romans killed eight and wounded twelve Zealots before they were slaughtered. When it was over, the Zealots gathered up their dead and took the caravan's wagons loaded with supplies. However, one of the soldiers who had been shot in the shoulder with an arrow and presumed dead by the Zealots was still alive. He stood, staggered, fell, got up, stumbling again and again throughout the cold night. The next afternoon he crawled into the garrison at Capernaum half-dead from the loss of blood.

A dozen or more soldiers scattered throughout the garrison relaxed in what little shade they could find. Two of the soldiers saw him and rushed over to give him some water. After swallowing a few sips of water the wounded soldier passed out. They carried him into one of the barracks and laid him on a cot. The arrow was removed from his shoulder and wrapped to stop the bleeding. Five hours later he regained consciousness and again was given some water to drink.

He slowly put his hand on his injured shoulder, wincing from the pain. He looked around with bloodshot eyes, saw a soldier and closed his eyes. "Tell your Captain . . . I . . . need to talk with him," he mumbled in a weak voice.

The soldier ran to tell Captain Drusus about the wounded soldier, stopping at the open door of Drusus' quarters to stand at attention. Drusus sat at his desk drinking a glass of wine, dressed in only his knee-length red shirt and leather sandals. His bleak quarters contained a bed, table and chair.

Drusus glanced at the soldier, leaned back in his chair and folded his massive arms in front of him. "What do you want?" he asked. His harsh voice left no doubt he disliked being disturbed.

Captain Marcus Drusus was a forty-two-year-old, highly intelligent, stern veteran in charge of three Roman legions in Galilee. He stood six feet tall, had piercing brown eyes, short dark hair, a beardless face and muscular build. He walked with a slight limp and had a deep, gruff voice.

"I'm sorry for the intrusion, Captain Drusus," the soldier answered, "but a badly injured soldier came crawling into the barracks last night. He passed out when we tried to give him some water. He only came to a few moments ago and asked to see you."

Drusus slid his chair back and rose to his feet with detectable irritation. He took a few steps toward the soldier who stepped back several steps. "Where is he now?" Drusus growled.

"He's in one of the barracks." Knowing better than to walk ahead of his captain, he waited for Drusus to be next to him. Then he pointed his finger and said, "This way, Captain."

They walked across the hot, dusty compound until they came to the barracks. The other soldiers in the barracks, seeing Drusus enter, sprang to their feet and stood at attention. Drusus saw the wounded soldier lying on a bunk. "At ease, men," he said. He walked over to the bunk and studied the unfamiliar face of the soldier. The wounded soldier opened his eyes and looked at Drusus. "You're not from one of my legions are you soldier?" Drusus asked.

The injured soldier tried to sit up but lacked the strength. His head fell back on his bunk. "No sir, I'm . . . from the ninth . . . legion stationed at Accho." He tried to clear his throat. "Captain Cassius sent fifty of us . . . with a caravan of supplies to Magdala. We were ambushed by . . . Jewish Zealots ten or so miles . . . before we got there."

Drusus looked at one of his men. "Bring him some water," Drusus said.

The soldier did as he was ordered. The wounded soldier sipped some water, closing his eyes. Then he opened his eyes. "I came here because I knew . . . this was closer . . . than Magdala. The Zealots assumed . . . I was dead along with . . . the rest of our men."

"Your captain was a fool for sending only fifty soldiers to protect a caravan on such a vital trip," Drusus said in disgust. "Either Captain Cassius was newly appointed by someone in Rome as a political favor and has no idea what he's doing, or Cassius underestimated the trouble the Zealots have been causing us here in Galilee recently. How many Jews do you think attacked you?"

The soldier's body had been wounded, *not* his ego. He had no intention of looking inept and exaggerated the number. "Over four hundred . . . at least."

Drusus looked at the nearest soldier. "Go find Sergeant Lucius. Tell him that I want to see him in my quarters at once!" Then he looked at the injured soldier. "I'll send word back to your idiot captain to tell him what happened to his men. I'll also inform those at Magdala not to expect their supplies, thanks to your captain."

With that, Drusus left for his quarters. It wasn't long before Sergeant Justin Lucius joined Drusus in his quarters. Lucius had been born and raised in Rome by his German parents after they had been brought there as captives many years earlier. So even though Lucius was in the Roman army and was Roman in many ways, he was really Germanic. He had blue eyes, light brown hair, stood six foot one and weighed a hundred eighty-three pounds.

"Sit down, Lucius, and have some wine," Drusus said. Lucius sat down, and poured a cup of wine. "God, I hate this awful heat!" Drusus complained, gulping down some wine. "I just had a disgusting conversation with a wounded soldier. He told me fifty soldiers were massacred by a band of four hundred Zealots while escorting supplies from Accho. The soldier said the attack took place around ten miles east of Magdala. I already sent a message to the soldier's idiot captain and another message to Magdala. I want you to take two cohorts and find the Zealots. If we're lucky, the supply wagons will have left tracks that you can follow. Bring back as many prisoners as you can. I want to crucify them as a public exhibition of what happens to bandits and insurrectionists."

Lucius finished his glass of wine, stood up and left without comment. *Drusus was optimistic in suggesting we might find the rebels,* he thought, walking toward the barracks. *He knows we've searched the hills and caves without discovering their whereabouts. Still, Drusus can't ignore the attack and has to try something no matter how unlikely the prospects.*

"Gabbiness, Captain Drusus wants two cohorts ready to march in three hours," Lucius told a fellow sergeant. "We're to find a band of four hundred Zealots that attacked a caravan. Tell the men to expect to be gone for five days."

*   *   *

For two exhausting, tedious days Lucius and eight hundred of his men combed the hills and caves under a hot sun, only to come up empty-handed. But on the third day one of Lucius' scouts, Diomedes, saw a dozen men riding horses across a plateau. They were less than half a mile in front of him and didn't see him. Even at that distance he could tell they were dressed like Jews. *The only Jews who have horses are those who have taken them from dead Romans,* he thought. Diomedes, realizing they must be Zealots, followed them. They rode several miles on the plateau that ran parallel to a range of hills. *I'll have a better chance of not being seen if I follow them from on top of the hill.* They went three more miles before going through a narrow gorge. Diomedes stopped, dismounted, ran down the hill and through the ravine. It

41

was less than two hundred yards long. He saw a large number of men, tents and horses scattered around an open field. He turned around and headed back to notify Lucius.

Half an hour later he caught up with Lucius. "Well, did you find anything?" Lucius asked, not expecting good news.

"I found out where the rebels are hiding. I followed them through a ravine that led into a secluded field."

"Thank all the gods," Lucius exclaimed. "It's about time we found their hiding place. I never thought we would. You did a great job, Diomedes. How far away was this ravine?"

"I would estimate between five or seven miles. The gorge is no more than two hundred yards long. There were dozens of tents and a corral for their horses. I didn't get a good look at the field but I didn't see any other way out. It looked like it was surrounded on all sides by steep cliffs."

"They must not have posted any lookouts on top of the cliff near the entrance or you would have been spotted. That's pretty stupid of them."

"Not necessarily, Sergeant," Diomedes replied. "I didn't want them to see me so I followed them from on top a ridge off to their left. When they went through the ravine I ran down to see where they went. I don't think a lookout could have seen me unless he was standing on the very edge of the cliff."

Lucius sighed. "That's too bad. In that case we better take it for granted they do have a lookout. Do you think you can find the gorge if we went around the other side of the hill you used to follow them?"

"Yes sir. I'll find it all right."

Lucius looked back at his men. Twenty officers had horses but seven hundred eighty men were on foot. They were already tired, hot, thirsty and hungry. He knew they wouldn't be in condition to march at least five miles to fight against men who were well rested.

Lucius looked at his second in command. "Gnaeus, I want you to tell the men that we found the rebels' hideout. We'll follow Diomedes and then make camp on the other side of the hill from their hideout. No one is to build a campfire. The rebels would see the light in the sky. Tell the men they'll have to eat cheese, dates and the remainder of their stale bread. We will attack first thing in the morning when the sun comes up. Not only will our men be well rested, the rebels will be less likely to expect an attack that early."

The men grumbled but were relieved they would be fighting the next morning instead of scouring the hills. Although the desert night was cold the soldiers were used to sleeping on the ground wrapped in blankets. A quarter moon didn't diminish the stars sparkling like millions of fireflies. Several times during the night a pack of wolves howled in the distance.

Lucius had a difficult time going to sleep as he usually did when anticipating a battle. His mind created all sorts of disasters where his men would be slaughtered. He strolled through the campsites to talk with anyone who might be awake. He found four men reminiscing about past campaigns. He sat down and joined in on their conversation.

Lucius was awake the next morning when the sky began to turn light blue and the stars disappeared. He kicked Gnaeus on the foot. "Tell the men to get ready. They'll have to go without eating. I want to catch the rebels before they are awake if possible. We'll not blow the horn to attack until they spot us or we're through the gorge."

Twenty minutes later Lucius' men moved out on empty stomachs. They were within a thousand yards of the ravine when a ram's horn blared out on top of a cliff. They had been seen.

"Sound the horn to attack!" Lucius yelled.

The horn sounded and the soldiers ran forward in a semi-orderly fashion. At the same time dozens of the Zealots scampered on top of a cliff to fire down on the soldiers with arrows. Lucius led his men through the ravine as arrows rained down like drops of rain at the start of a storm. Hitting a running target from high above was difficult, but seven soldiers were killed and another nineteen wounded before making it through the gorge. Once most of the soldiers were through the ravine the battle was ferocious. The Zealots fought to the death, knowing if they survived they would be crucified. The Zealots were outnumbered four to one. Eleven wounded Zealots were taken alive and over two hundred dead were left to rot in the sun. Three of the wounded rebels died on the way to Capernaum.

Lucius and his exhausted men entered the garrison three hours before sunset. After the remaining eight Zealots were thrown into prison Lucius went straight to Drusus' quarters with mixed feelings. He believed Rome would one day rule the world in peace under one supreme ruler, and was willing to fight to make that dream a reality. Yet, he hated slaughtering people who resisted Rome's might.

Drusus watched Lucius walk in, pour a cup of wine, and collapse on a chair. Lucius wiped the sweat off his brow, and drank some wine. "We finally found one of the camps and killed more than two hundred of them. All together, we lost nineteen of our own men with another twenty-three wounded." Lucius didn't sound happy.

Drusus leaned back and smiled. "Well, well, well. Congratulations my old friend. When word about that gets around it should discourage the Jews from committing treason. I must confess that I didn't think you had much chance of finding them. I take it you were able to follow the wagons' tracks."

"We did for several miles until they disappeared on rocky ground. We spent two days searching the hills without finding anything. On the third day Diomedes was out scouting ahead of us and saw a band of Jews riding horses. He followed them to their hiding place. He came back and led us there. You can guess the rest."

Drusus, puzzled by Lucius' expression, asked, "Why the gloomy look on your face? That's the kind of expression I would expect if you said you never found them."

Lucius stared at his cup of wine. "I guess I'm just tired. Many of the men we killed were barely more than boys. I saw the terror in their eyes as we cut them down. It was different when we fought armies in the past. This wasn't an army."

"Maybe they weren't what you consider an army, Lucius, but such *boys* as you described are capable of killing soldiers. Our job is to bring these stubborn people in line. If they choose to allow their young men to fight against us, so be it. Did you bring back any captives?"

Lucius knew what Drusus had in mind. "Yes. We put eight of them in prison."

"Listen, Lucius, we've been friends for more than ten years. I can tell by your expression that you'd prefer not to crucify the prisoners. But I'm convinced if we *don't* crucify the rebels it might make the Jews think they can get away with rebellion. I want you to crucify the prisoners along the road into the city first thing in the morning."

The next morning Lucius led the eight prisoners outside the city. Three of them carried the beam used to crucify them but the other five were too weak. The eight rebels were crucified about a hundred yards apart. They screamed when the nails were driven into their wrists but passed out from the pain. When they finished Lucius went back to his quarters and drank wine until he passed out. He knew he would wake up, unlike the crucified prisoners.

*   *   *

It was over a week since the eight prisoners had been crucified. Instead of their deaths decreasing the opposition to Rome, it had the reverse effect. The Zealots attracted more and more men to their cause. One of the men who had been crucified, Conaniah, had two brothers, Pelaiah and Hariph.

Zedekiah approached Hariph who was selling wool in his shop. "I was sorry to hear about Conaniah," Zedekiah said. "He was a good man and a valiant patriot."

"My brother, Pelaiah, thinks he was a fool," Hariph replied.

"What do *you* think?"

"I think Pelaiah is a coward."

"Pelaiah!" Zedekiah said in surprise. "I don't believe it. He's never been afraid in his life."

"He didn't used to be, but that was before he started following a rabbi called Jesus. This rabbi convinced Pelaiah we should love our enemies. It's the stupidest thing I ever heard."

"I don't see how Pelaiah could think that after Conaniah was crucified. Maybe Pelaiah has changed his mind. Have you talked with him since your brother was crucified?"

"Yes, but he still feels the same way. Pelaiah said we must forgive our enemies. That was another thing Jesus told him. I tell you, Zedekiah, I'll *never* forgive the Romans! I despise Pelaiah *and* Jesus."

Zedekiah glanced behind him to see if anyone could hear him. "I don't blame you, but the Romans are the ones you should hate," he whispered. "How would you like to join the Zealots and fight them the way Conaniah did?"

"I would."

"Good. I'll come to your house after you close your shop to take you to a meeting we're having." Zedekiah turned to walk away, stopping to look back at Hariph. "Better not tell Pelaiah. He might be crazy enough to betray you."

*   *   *

The sixth day of the week was the Jewish Sabbath, a Holy Day when Jews were prohibited by their religious law from traveling and working. It lasted from sunset on Friday to sunset on Saturday to honor the day when God rested after creation. It also was the *sign* of the Covenant God had made with Moses on Mount Sinai. If a Jew violated one of the strict rules attached to the Sabbath he faced death by stoning.

On this particular Sabbath, Gideon talked with Harim in private as they sat under the shade of a cypress tree, enjoying a slight breeze. The rest of their family relaxed inside the house. "Have you heard about a new rabbi who some people claim has performed miracles?" Gideon asked.

Harim looked at him with a curious expression. "Yes, I heard about such a man. Why do you want to know that?"

"My friends and I happened to follow a crowd of people who were listening to a man called Jesus. I overheard one of them say he might be the Messiah. When we told Elizabad's father about it, he said Jesus heals people. If Jesus is the Messiah he might heal Jehoram." He instantly felt guilty for not adding their father already told him to stop thinking about the new rabbi.

Gideon was about to tell him but Harim spoke first. "Listen, Gideon, *if* this man was the Messiah he would destroy the Romans and become king, not go around healing the sick. The Messiah is supposed to use God's power to free his people from oppression. From what I heard this Jesus spends all his time hanging around weak and helpless people. What kind of king is that?"

"True, but the Messiah will need followers if he is to become king. He might heal people to demonstrate his power in order to draw others to his side."

Harim smiled at what he thought was his young brother's naivety. "That makes sense except for one thing. If what you said were *true* he would do so in Jerusalem, not up here in Galilee. The Messiah will be King David's son and Jerusalem was David's capital."

Gideon lowered his head in disappointment. Harim put his hand on Gideon's shoulder. "I know how much you want

Jehoram to be healed," Harim said. "Tell you what I'll do. I'll ask around and find out all I can about this rabbi. How's that?"

"I'd really appreciate that Harim." Gideon started to get up but sat back down, staring at the ground in front of him. "Please don't tell father that I asked you about Jesus. I already talked with father about Jesus, and he told me to forget all about him."

Harim patted Gideon on his knee. "Don't worry about my keeping our secret from father," Harim said, smiling. "I promise you that this will remain between only the two of us."

Meanwhile, Jesus sat with his disciples in an olive grove not far from one of his disciple's mother-in-law's home in Capernaum, teaching them about the Kingdom of God by telling parables. "The Kingdom of God is like a man who sowed good seed in his field. But when he was sleeping, his enemies came and sowed weeds among the wheat, and went away. When the wheat spouted and formed heads, the weeds also appeared. The owner's servants came to him, and said, 'Sir, didn't you sow good seed in your field? Where did the weeds come from?' The owner said, 'An enemy did this.' The servants asked, 'Do you want us to pull them out?' 'No,' the owner answered, 'because you will pull up the wheat with them. At the time of the harvest, I will tell the harvesters to collect the weeds and tie them into bundles to be burned. Then gather the wheat and bring it into my barn.'"

A neighbor rushed up to them in a state of panic. He caught his breath, and said, "Peter, you'd better come right away! Your mother-in-law was preparing a meal when she suddenly became dizzy, and collapsed on the floor. We put her on her bed, and sent for a doctor. But by the time he arrived she was unconscious. He said he couldn't help her. No one knows what's wrong with her."

Peter jumped to his feet. "Teacher, I must go see what has happened to my mother-in-law. Tell me where you will be going and I'll join you as soon as possible."

Jesus stood up, and replied in a calm voice, "That will not be necessary, Peter. We'll go with you to your mother-in-law's home."

They didn't have far to go, but Peter felt like it was taking forever to get there. Friends and neighbors met them at the door with tears in their eyes. One of the women looked at Peter. "Sir, your mother-in-law is near death," she said, sobbing. "The doctor was here but left when he knew he couldn't help her. Would you like for us to send for the priest?"

Peter glanced at Jesus but didn't say anything. Jesus walked into the bedroom and touched Peter's mother-in-law gently on the hand. She slowly opened her eyes, and asked with a bewildered expression, "Sir, why are you here?"

Jesus smiled as he helped her to her feet. "You were sick but now you are well. You may join your friends."

She was confused why there were so many people in her home, but began to serve them. Her guests were even more confused and astonished than she was. Another one of Jesus' followers, Phillip, pulled Peter aside. "What exactly did Jesus do, Peter?"

"He touched her hand and she woke up. I saw and heard nothing else. We saw him cast out an evil spirit yesterday, and now this. He *must* be the promised Messiah! What I don't understand is why he always insists we not tell anyone when everyone seems to hear about it anyway."

As they were leaving a young man ran up to Jesus, trying to catch his breath. "Rabbi, I bring . . . troubling news from Jerusalem. Herod Antipas has . . . thrown John the Baptist . . . into prison." He took a deep breath. "Many Jews in Judea are angry . . . and have threatened to storm . . . the prison to free him. All they need is someone to lead them. You, and your followers here in Galilee . . . combined with John's followers in Judea . . . could be that man."

"No, our friend John was born to prepare the way for the Kingdom of God," Jesus replied. "He has done so. The work John was given by God wasn't to destroy either Herod or Rome. Don't be concerned for John. He is in God's hands."

"Do you think Jesus meant that God will free John by a miracle?" Matthew asked Andrew.

Andrew shrugged his shoulders. "I don't know. It sounded like it but I know better than trying to guess what Jesus means. All we can do is wait and see."

*   *   *

Jesus wasn't the only person who had received word about John the Baptist's arrest. So had Drusus. He grinned slyly as he talked with Lucius over some wine in his quarters. "It appears that fool Herod Antipas is having problems with the Jews in Jerusalem." He sounded delighted. "Good, I never did like it when Caesar allowed Herod the Great and his descendents to remain as kings. Instead of these kings placating the people, they cause more trouble than they're worth."

"Why is Herod in trouble? What has the idiot done now?"

"He tossed one of their so-called prophets in prison." Drusus laughed. "This one is really a strange character who goes around in smelly rags, eats locust, and dunks people in water. He calls it baptism, whatever that means. A man they call John the Baptist. It's some kind of religious ritual. Herod didn't mind as long as the man drowned people in water and talked about repenting. But then this John began to preach against Herod for marrying his half-brother's wife, Herodias."

"What's wrong with that?" Lucius asked.

"Herod had divorced his wife. It's against Jewish religious law for a man to divorce his wife in order to marry someone else. From what I've heard this Herodias is a very vindictive woman. She's the one who insisted that Herod arrest the irritating prophet. Whatever happens to the prophet, you can bet she is behind it."

Lucius laughed. "It sounds to me like she and Herod deserve each other. What do you think they will do with this prophet?"

"I have no idea."

"What difference would it make to Caesar what happens to this troublemaker?" Lucius asked.

"John the Baptist is very popular with the Jews. I hope there might be enough fuss over his arrest to attract the attention of Caesar. Maybe even enough for Caesar to get rid of those Herods for good, and allow the Roman governors to rule on their own."

"I take it you're not worried a rebellion over this prophet's arrest might spread to our region as well?"

"That's not very likely," Drusus answered, grinning. "For one thing their anger is directed at their own Jewish king, *not* Rome. For another it has to do with their religion, and not our taxes for a change. Besides, there are more than enough prophets here in Galilee to distract the attention of the Jews away from one crackpot in Judea. I've heard of one by the name of Jesus. He's causing quite a stir among the religious leaders. Let the Jews worry about him if they want."

Lucius didn't share Drusus' confidence about rebellion not spreading north, but didn't argue the point. He tugged at the leather-strap over his shoulders that held his breastplate, and was biting into his skin. "I've never been to Judea, but I know you have a number of times," Lucius said. "I understand the Jews there are even more stubborn than those here. What did you think of Judea?"

"I hated it! It's mostly a harsh, barren land, and even hotter there than here. Worse, many of the people either refuse or don't know how to speak Greek. They only talk in Hebrew. You try dealing with people who don't understand a word you're saying."

*   *   *

The Sabbath ended when the sun set in the western sky. Rachel went to her small bedroom on the second floor. She lay on her bed, and closed her eyes. Feeling melancholy over not being married, she wondered if she would ever marry. She discovered her mother's advice wasn't easy to follow. Rachel had agreed it was for the best to forget about her Roman protector, but she couldn't forget the soldier with the kind eyes. She remembered his mother's exact words. *"Not only is there little chance you might meet him again, he probably wouldn't recognize you if he did."*

Yet, her mind wasn't able to exorcise the thought of the soldier who had befriended her. She felt foolish and forlorn for not being able to forget about him. *Why should he remember me? I deliberately concealed my face from the soldiers.* She rolled over, closed her eyes, and tried in vain to go to sleep. She sat up when it suddenly dawned on her that his eyes were not brown like the other Romans. They were *blue. Maybe that's why I noticed his eyes in the first place.* She plopped back down on her pillow. *I wonder if he isn't even Roman?*

Chapter Four

The next morning was hot even before the sun slowly peeked over the eastern hills of Galilee. Drusus dunked his head into a bucket of water when he heard a soldier knock on his open door. Drusus shook his head, and ran his hands through his hair. He glared at the soldier. "What do you want?" he asked.

"There's a Jew outside who wants to talk with you in private. He refuses to give his name."

"Does he now?" Drusus grumbled, sitting down behind his desk. "Tell him to come in."

A thin man in a red cloak draped over his knee-length tunic came in, bowing his head. He appeared to be in his mid-thirties. Drusus stared at him for several minutes before speaking. "What's your name?" he finally asked.

"My name is unimportant, but what I came to tell you isn't. Suffice it to say that I want to bring peace to our land. I'm what some would call a prophet, or if you prefer, a seer. I see the future through dreams and visions."

Drusus laughed. "I prefer to call such people crazy. So, what do you see in *your* future? Being lashed out the gate?"

"If you wish, but first let me tell about a dream I had last night."

Whoever this man is, he isn't afraid, Drusus thought.

The visitor closed his eyes, and spoke as if he was in a trance. *"I stood before a man I did not know. My eyes glass, my breath wind, my heart panted and my limbs shook. My body rose above the ground as if I had been seized by my hair and borne aloft. The man didn't speak, but put his thoughts into my mind. I realized the man before me was more than a man. He would go before me, and I would follow his footsteps. He drew strength from a source I did not recognize."*

Drusus tugged his earlobe, wondering if the man really could see into the future. "What did you make out of this remarkable dream of yours?" he asked.

"In the past, my dreams have often been symbolic. In such dreams and visions things are not what they seem on the surface. I took the *man who was more than a man* to be Rome. His strength I understood to be the Roman army. His purpose is to bring peace to my people."

"So why did you come here to tell me this?"

"The only way to bring peace to Galilee is to put a stop to the slaughter brought about by the Zealots. The dream meant Rome will rule the entire world, and the army will be the means to that end. I want to help you put an end to the Zealots before more of my countrymen are killed."

Drusus slouched back in his chair, and folded his arms in front of him. "How do you plan on doing that?"

"I will tell you who they are and where you can find them. I don't do this with a glad heart, Captain, but it will bring peace in the end. I want no money or recognition from Rome. That's why I didn't tell you my name."

Drusus stood up. "I understand and will respect your wish. Bring me what information you have when you have it. No one will know anything about it. Not even my own men. This will be between the two of us."

Drusus watched the man walk out the garrison. He motioned for the soldier who brought him there to come toward him. He pointed to the stranger. "Whenever you see that man enter the garrison I want you to bring him straight to me. Don't let anyone stop him, and don't ask him any questions."

*   *   *

The next morning Rachel helped her mother prepare the family's breakfast of salted fish, pomegranates, honey and sliced bread. After eating, they all performed their duties for the morning. Rachel milked their goat, Sarah made soap, Gideon picked apples, and Harim sharpened several tools. When they were finished, Elhanan made his way to their boat with Harim and Gideon.

"May I go to Martha's now?" Rachel asked her mother.

Sarah didn't answer, noticing Jehoram was still sitting at the table. "Are you feeling all right, Jehoram?" she asked. "Your face looks pale."

"I feel sick and my stomach hurts," he answered, folding his arms over his lower belly.

"I think you should go to bed and stay there until you feel better." Sarah glanced at Rachel, and whispered, "Go get Pildash. He'll know what to do."

Rachel ran to fetch Pildash. He had been trained by a Greek in medicine, and knew as much about it as anyone in Capernaum. It didn't take long for him to accompany Rachel to her house. Sarah and Rachel stood behind him while he examined Jehoram. They were worried, not curious.

Pildash sat on the edge of Jehoram's bed. He looked into Jehoram's eyes, felt his forehead and then pushed down on his stomach. When he abruptly released the pressure Jehoram laughed and said, "That tickles."

"Good," Pildash said, rising to his feet. Turning toward Sarah, he said, "I don't think there's anything serious wrong with him. It must have been something he ate. Try to get him to drink some sour milk or sour wine. It will make him empty his stomach."

Meanwhile, Elhanan, Harim and Gideon were almost to their boat when they saw a noisy commotion near the water's edge. They and three other fishermen rushed over to see what was going on. When they got there several fishermen stood over the body of a Roman soldier they had just pulled out of the water.

A Phoenician fisherman rolled him over, and jumped back with a terrified expression. "He been stabbed!" he gasped. "God protect us! The Romans will blame us for this."

Elhanan gave a quick glance at Harim who was as bewildered as everyone else. Elhanan sighed with relief, certain that his son had no knowledge of what had happened. No one had to spell out what this murder would most likely mean. The confusion and fear was contagious.

An older fisherman said, "We better inform the Roman garrison about this."

"Don't be a fool!" another man snapped angrily. "If we tell them about a murdered soldier we'll all be arrested. They won't care who was responsible. They will punish the innocent along with the guilty like they always do. I say we should take the body up into the hills and bury him."

Several other fishermen echoed their agreement. "The Romans might not find the body, and even if they do they might not connect it with us," one man said.

They argued back and forth. Two fishermen started to shove each other around. Elhanan and his sons listened to the frightened men voice their opinions. Then Elhanan raised his hands. "Listen to me for a minute!" he pleaded. "Even if the body isn't discovered, it won't take long for the Romans to miss one of their comrades. It doesn't matter if they find the body or not, our neighbors will still be blamed for his death."

"But at least it won't be one of us!" a terrified fisherman shouted.

"You don't know that, and you don't mean it!" Elhanan said in a forceful voice. "I understand why you're afraid, but think for a minute before you do something foolish. This man was obviously killed during our Sabbath. The Romans know we never travel far from our homes on the Sabbath. They'll realize the killer couldn't have been a Jew, but must have been killed by a soldier or some other Gentile. If we report this at once it will convince them we have nothing to hide."

The panicky fishermen were hotly divided in their opinions as to what to do. Finally, Elhanan said, "I'll personally report this man's death to the Roman garrison. None of you need come."

The same fisherman who had suggested taking to body to the garrison spoke up. "If you are willing to risk your life, Elhanan, the rest of us will share our day's catch of fish with you. That way you won't lose out on the day's catch."

Everyone seemed agreeable to both Elhanan's suggestion and the fisherman's proposal except for Harim. "That's not fair!" he protested in disgust. "My father risks his life, while you go fishing."

"It was your father's idea, Harim, not ours." a different fisherman replied.

Harim looked at his father. "Don't do this thing, Father, or you'll surely be arrested no matter how persuasive you are. You know Rome doesn't wait for explanations when they have a Jew already in their cruel hands."

Elhanan reached out and took his son's arm. "I know how much you hate the Romans, Harim, but they'll want to catch the real killer. After all, it was a Roman soldier who was killed, not a Jew."

Harim didn't want to admit his father was right, but what he had said about the victim was true. The fact that it was one of their soldiers who was killed did make a difference. Harim knew there wasn't anything he could say to change his father's resolve. "Then at least allow me to go with you," Harim said in frustration.

Elhanan didn't want Harim to go with him, but if it was as safe as he had insisted, he had no reason to deny Harim's request. "All right, Harim, but don't loose your temper and say something to make matters worse."

Elhanan looked at Gideon and put his hand on his shoulder. "I want you to go home, Gideon, and tell your mother what has happened. Tell her not to worry. I'll come straight home after we report the soldier's murder to the commander of the garrison. Be sure to tell your mother the other fishermen will divide their catch with me."

Gideon ran home to tell his mother what had happened. When he arrived home, Jehoram sat outside working on his boat. Pildash's remedy had worked. Rachel was scrubbing carrots as Sarah removed freshly baked bread from the brick oven. They were surprised to see Gideon walk into the house, huffing and puffing. They could tell he was excited about something.

"Why aren't you out fishing with your father and brother?" Sarah asked in alarm, not as a reprimand.

Gideon took a deep breath, and answered between gasps. "When we arrived . . . at the dock some fishermen . . . pulled a dead soldier . . . out of the water."

Rachel's face turned white, and she dropped a carrot. She put her hand on Gideon's shoulder. "A dead soldier! Can you describe him?"

Sarah glanced at her daughter with a sour expression. She knew why Rachel asked her question, but didn't say anything in front of Gideon and Jehoram. "Well," Gideon answered, "he was stiff as a board when they lifted him out of the water. His face was white as a sheet and badly wrinkled. He was about father's age, and very skinny. His helmet was missing and I noticed that he was bald. Why do you want to know?"

Rachel felt her mother staring at her in disapproval. "No reason," she answered, "just curious, that's all." She may or may not have fooled Gideon, but she was certain she hadn't deceived her mother.

Gideon, puzzled by his sister's enigmatic answer thought, *Curious about a dead soldier?* He said, "Anyway, Father and Harim went to the Roman garrison to tell them about the dead soldier. Father told me to let you know the other fishermen promised to divide today's catch with him. He also said he will come straight home after that."

There were two things on Sarah's mind. First and foremost, fear for Elhanan and Harim. Second, Rachel's obvious preoccupation for the soldier she had talked about. Sarah looked at Gideon. "As long as you're not going fishing today, Gideon, you can chop some wood. When you're finished with that, I want you to take Jehoram for a walk. He was feeling sick earlier and I think a little exercise will do him good."

After Gideon and Jehoram were gone, Sarah confronted Rachel. "You lied to Gideon, but I saw the expression on your face when he mentioned a dead soldier. You still have some foolhardy fantasy of meeting the one who helped you, don't you?"

Rachel walked over to the open door and watched Gideon and Jehoram making their way down the road. "Not really, Mother." Rachel turned, and looked at her mother with a single tear in one eye. "I know that you were right when I first told you about him. Nothing can come out of a chance meeting with a man I never spoke with or know anything about. But yes, I admit that for an instant I was afraid he might be dead."

Sarah took a few steps toward Rachel, put her arms around her and hugged her. "I know it hasn't been very easy on you these last years since your fiancé died." She released Rachel, and looked into her moist eyes. "You look at Martha's young sons and long to have a family of your own. Believe me, I can understand how you feel. But you must be patient, Rachel. God will provide you with a fine husband and family but he will be Jewish, not a Roman."

Rachel wiped her eyes as she sat down at the table. "I know. I've tried to forget him but it's been very hard to get his face out of my mind. I even see him in my dreams."

*　　*　　*

Herod's palace had been built to convey wealth and prestige. The spacious rooms were decorated with tapestries from Rome, Egypt and Persia. The king's meals were in the hands of the finest cooks and were served by servants on gold or silver plates. The meals were often accompanied with music, excessive drinking, and dancers in extravagant costumes, followed by entertainment, games or gambling.

On the other hand, Roman garrisons were meant to convey a different sort of message altogether. Stark in comparison to the palace, they represented strength, not wealth and comfort. The cold, bare walls of thick stone were formidable. The towers were meant for battle, not to provide a view of the scenery. Like Rome itself, the garrisons seemed impregnable.

When Elhanan and Harim approached the open large, wooden-gates they were stopped by two armed guards. One glared at Elhanan. "What do you want?" he asked, his tone harsh and confrontational.

"We'd like to talk with the man in charge," Elhanan answered.

Harim was stunned his father seemed so calm. He always assumed his father was afraid of soldiers. Harim, remembering his father's stern warning to keep his mouth shut, didn't speak.

The guard laughed and looked at the other guard. "So you want to see the man in charge, do you?" He looked at Elhanan. "What makes you think *he* would be interested in talking with two Jews?"

Harim saw six or seven other soldiers scattered throughout the courtyard inside the garrison. He felt his hatred burning like an open fire inside his stomach. "Because we are here to report a murder, that's why," Elhanan answered. He deliberately spoke loud enough for several of the other soldiers to hear. His words caught their attention just as Elhanan had expected.

The guard took several steps toward Elhanan, his eyes glaring with rage. Harim clenched his fists when the guard pointed his sword at Elhanan. "If you think our captain will be interested in hearing that a soldier killed a Jew, forget it," the guard growled.

"I doubt your captain will want to forget it when I tell him that it was a soldier, not a Jew, who was murdered," Elhanan replied. "Now, do we get to see him or not?"

The guard, astonished a Jew would wish to report the murder of a soldier, was baffled by Elhanan's courage. He lowered his sword, and took a moment to study Elhanan's face with suspicion. Then he said, "Follow me."

He led them through the gate into the spacious courtyard. They walked passed three pits with lambs roasting over the fires. Some of the soldiers stared at Elhanan and Harim as they followed the guard toward Drusus' quarters. Harim's fists were still clenched.

There are no pleasant sounds of children laughing, or women humming cheerfully, or fountains spouting water into the air, Elhanan thought. *It's a stark and bleak setting the soldiers call home.*

Elhanan and Harim followed the guard to Captain Drusus' quarters, stopping outside the open door. "These two Jews said they wanted to report that a soldier has been murdered," the guard announced. When he said *Jews* his voice sounded condescending.

Drusus sat at his desk counting out stacks of silver coins. The coins were the month's wages for the soldiers. He glanced at Elhanan with a sour expression. "Who are you and where did you find his body?"

"I'm Elhanan, son of Benjamin. This is my oldest son, Harim. We found the body by the water's edge when we were on our way to our fishing boat. His body was stiff, white and badly wrinkled. It was clear he had been dead for one day. We assumed his body had been washed ashore."

Drusus rose, walked within a few feet of Elhanan and stared directly into his eyes. "What made you think he was murdered rather than drowned?"

"There were multiple stab wounds on his back. We left the body where we found it. We realized you would want to examine it yourself. Besides, our religious law prohibits us from touching a dead body. A Phoenician had pulled him out of the water and turned him over. I can take you there if you want me to."

Drusus continued to stare into Elhanan's eyes. "You're either very stupid or brave to come here to tell me all this. What makes you think we won't blame you for killing him?"

"I doubt a murderer would risk coming to you to report his own crime. We came here because we didn't want you to start arresting our neighbors for a murder they obviously didn't commit."

Drusus squinted his eyes in skepticism, still staring at Elhanan. "Maybe you're not stupid after all, but are extremely clever. Clever enough in fact to think that by coming here we'd assume you must be innocent. And why did you say it was obvious your neighbors didn't commit the murder?"

"I'm neither clever nor brave," Elhanan replied. "The reason why I said it was obvious my neighbors were innocent is because the soldier *must* have killed on the Sabbath. I'm sure you know Jews don't go from their house on our Holy Day."

Drusus walked back to his chair, sat down and smiled. "Well, Elhanan, son of Benjamin, you claim that you aren't brave or clever but I think you must be. However, my impression is that you are telling the truth." He glanced at the guard, and ordered, "Tell Lucius I want to see him." He looked at back at Elhanan. "When my sergeant gets here I want you to go with him and show him where the body is. While we wait, you can tell me about yourself. I find you a most interesting man. You already indicated you're a fisherman when you mentioned you were on your way to your boat."

Harim was dumbfounded the Roman captain accepted his father's explanation so readily, and now seemed cordial. Elhanan, sensing his son's confusion over Drusus' unexpected pleasant manner, was delighted Harim was there to witness it.

Elhanan put his hand on Harim's shoulder. "I already said this is my oldest son, Harim. I also have two other sons, Gideon and Jehoram. I have one daughter, Rachel. My wife's name is Sarah. We've lived in Capernaum all our lives. My family have been fishermen for over five generations."

Before Elhanan could say more, Lucius arrived. "I was told you wanted to see me, Captain." He glanced at Elhanan and Harim, but didn't comment on their presence.

"Lucius, these two men brought word of a murdered soldier," Drusus replied. Elhanan and Harim noticed he referred to them as *men,* not as Jews. "I want you to take six of your men, and go with them to bring the dead soldier. Four of the men can bring the body here while you and two soldiers see if you can learn anything. And make sure your men treat our friends here with respect, understand?"

Drusus looked at Elhanan with a broad grin. "Thank you for coming here to tell me about our soldier, Elhanan, son of Benjamin."

They were halfway to the gate when Lucius let out a cheerful laugh, taking Elhanan and Harim by surprise.

"Captain Drusus must have been impressed about something you said or did, that's for sure," Lucius said. "He usually tries to act more ferocious. Yet, he really isn't the bully most of the soldiers think he is. I guess I'm the only one he shows any friendship towards. I saved his life once when we were fighting in Gaul."

"To tell you the truth, I was quite impressed by your captain, too," Elhanan replied.

Harim detested Drusus and Lucius for their friendly manner. He wanted his father to despise the Romans, but their display of affability was making that less likely. He sighed in disgust. *I hope none of my friends see us with seven Roman soldiers walking along in each other's company like good friends. Especially when father is laughing and talking so cheerfully with Lucius.*

Elhanan was pleased Harim was seeing a different side of the Romans than the one he felt all Romans had. Elhanan knew Harim was listening, when he speculated warmly, "I imagine it must be a lonely life living in a foreign country."

"It is when the people hate you as much as we're hated here," Lucius answered, smiling. "Most of the other people we rule eventually grow to accept us, but not here in the east."

"I couldn't help but notice that you don't look Roman," Elhanan said.

"I'm not. My parents were German, but I was born and raised in Rome. My parents were brought to Italy as captives after three Roman legions were massacred in Germany."

"I hope you don't mind my asking, but why are you willing to be a Roman soldier when your parents were slaves?" Elhanan asked.

Lucius laughed. "They weren't never *slaves,* Elhanan. They soon were given their freedom and became successful farmers. Rome's policy is to incorporate other nationalities into the empire. That would happen here if your people would allow it."

Harim wanted to scream, "Liar!" but held his tongue.

They arrived at the shore where the body lay in the sand like a dead fish. "There's your man, Sergeant Lucius," Elhanan said. "Like I told Captain Drusus, Jews can't touch a dead body, but a Phoenician fisherman turned him over. It was then we noticed the soldier had been stabbed."

Elhanan and Harim left the Romans to attend to their duty, while they headed for home. Neither of them had anything to say about their experience. Elhanan hoped Harim had mellowed in his feelings toward Rome. Sarah, worried sick waiting for them to return home, saw them coming up the dusty road.

"They're home," she cried, jumping off her chair to run out to meet them. She hugged Elhanan and asked, "What happened at the garrison? When Gideon told me where you were going, I was terrified."

"I'll tell you all about it in the house," Elhanan replied, putting his arm around Sarah's waist. "It wasn't quite what I expected."

Harim had no desire to review the experience he had detested. He believed even though Drusus and Lucius seemed friendly it didn't alter the fact that Romans usually treated Jews with brutality. He was convinced that given another opportunity, they undoubtedly would be just as cruel. "I think I'll go for a walk," he grumbled.

Elhanan and Sarah walked into the house where their other three children waited anxiously. Elhanan poured a cup of wine, drank it straight down, poured another and sat down. He took a deep breath and let it out. "We were almost to our boat when we saw two fishermen pulling a soldier out of the water. A Phoenician turned him over and said the soldier had been stabbed. Needless to say, everyone was terrified of what the Romans would do. They argued back and forth as what to do. Some wanted to bury him in the hills, but others thought we should notify the Romans. Anyway, I finally said I would go to the garrison to report the murder. Harim objected and tried to talk me out of it, but when I refused he asked if he could go with me."

He drank some wine as Sarah, Gideon, Rachel and Jehoram watched and listened in fascination. "When Harim and I reached the gate two guards stopped us and said their captain wouldn't want to talk with us. They changed their minds after I told them a soldier had been murdered. The captain's name is Drusus. At first he was skeptical of my story, which wasn't a surprise. But it didn't take long for him to change his mind. I was glad Harim had insisted to go with me. Drusus was reasonable and rather friendly. I could tell Harim was stunned by it."

"He didn't say anything to get into trouble, did he?" Sarah asked.

"He didn't say anything at all, but I knew he was befuddled. Anyway, Drusus sent a soldier to fetch a sergeant called Lucius. While we waited Drusus asked me about our family. He was polite and seemed interested. He ordered Lucius to go with us to get the dead soldier. On the way, Lucius talked with us like good friends. Again, I could tell Harim was puzzled by it all. I thank God he was there to see it."

"Do you think it might change the way he feels?" Sarah asked in a hopeful voice.

"I pray that it does. If he thinks about it long enough with an open mind, it might." Elhanan took Sarah's hand. "To be honest with you, Sarah, our witnessing the prisoners being led through the street left a powerful impression on him. Today's experience might not be enough to erase it." He finished his wine. "How were things around here?"

"Jehoram felt sick shortly after you left," Sarah answered, smiling at Jehoram. "Pildash came and examined him. He said he thought it was something he ate. He told us to give him sour milk or wine to empty his stomach. I gave him sour milk. Jehoram hated the taste but rid himself of his food."

"It tasted terrible, but I felt better," Jehoram said. "I finished my boat, Father. Want to see it?"

"I most certainly do," Elhanan answered with a proud smile. "Where is it?"

Jehoram pushed himself up, hopped outside and returned with the boat. "Here it is," he said, handing it to his father. "Like it?"

Elhanan held it up in the air to admire it. "It's a splendid boat, Jehoram. It looks just like mine. Congratulations. What will you make next?"

"I want to make a model of the temple but you'll have to find a piece of wood for me."

Gideon burst out, "I can do that for you!"

Chapter Five

The next morning, half a dozen fishermen greeted Elhanan, Harim and Gideon at the dock. "What happened when you and Harim went to the Roman garrison?" one of them asked.

The fishermen gathered around Elhanan like excited children waiting to hear about some fantastic adventure. Harim gritted his teeth as he got into the boat to make ready to sail. Gideon listened along with the fishermen to his father tell his story once again.

"There's not much to tell," Elhanan said. "When a guard at the gate took us to Captain Drusus' quarters I told him that we found a dead soldier near the water. At first he was skeptical of my story but then he believed me. Drusus sent for a Sergeant Lucius. While we waited Drusus asked me about my family. Then we took Lucius to the dead man. I must say the garrison is a grim place to live."

The fishermen were relieved the Romans were willing to accept Elhanan's account, and *surprised* the Romans weren't more hostile toward Elhanan. When Elhanan finished telling them what they wanted to know, the same fisherman who had promised him a fair share of the previous day's catch handed Elhanan a small leather pouch.

"Here's your portion of yesterday's catch, Elhanan," he said. "A shekel and three drachmas. You certainly earned it!"

Elhanan thanked him, and dropped the pouch in the front of the boat. He and Gideon joined Harim in their boat. Elhanan knew why Harim was sullen and quiet. His oldest son was still perplexed by how they had been treated by the Romans. Elhanan *hoped* that some of Harim's hatred was softening now that he had personally experienced that the Romans actually wanted justice, not just revenge against an innocent Jew.

Gideon, oblivious of all this, said brightly, "The water is really calm today. We should do well fishing if it stays this way."

They had moderate success for several hours until an unexpected wind picked up, making the waves so strong it was difficult to control their net. Their boat rocked back and forth, the sea splashing into the boat. This was a frequent occurrence and Elhanan decided to wait for a while to see if the wind would let up. After half-an-hour, it subsided enough to resumed fishing. But they didn't do nearly as well.

At home, Sarah worried the Romans might blame Elhanan for the murder if they weren't able to find out who was the real killer. Rachel sat at the table mending one of Gideon's shirts, sensing her mother's anxiety. She wondered if it was due to her infatuation with the Roman soldier. "What's troubling you, Mother?" she asked.

Sarah stopped slicing cheese, and sat down on the opposite side of the table. "I'm frightened the soldiers might come to arrest your father," she answered. "When he told us about his meeting with their captain your father seemed pleased by the captain's friendliness, but I feel your father might have overestimated his fairness. If they don't find out who killed that Roman soon, the captain might decide to make an example out of your father. He might think that it's better to arrest a Jew than allow a murderer get away with killing a soldier."

Rachel stared at her mother. "Do you really think they would do such a thing?"

"Absolutely! The Romans have no qualms about arresting an innocent Jew as an example to warn others from doing something."

Rachel rose and walked over to put her arms around her mother. "Don't cry, Mother, don't cry. You know father is always a good judge of a man's real character. He felt that the captain could be trusted to do the right thing." In spite of her attempt to assure her mother, Rachel worried that her mother's fear might have been right.

*   *   *

For the next two days the Roman soldiers went door to door, questioning the residents of Capernaum about whether or not they heard or saw anything that might have been a fight between a soldier and another man. The atmosphere in the city was dreadful. People were terrified the Romans might come to place them under arrest.

Neither Sarah nor Rachel mentioned a thing to Elhanan about their growing fear that he might be in danger. Sarah thought it likely Elhanan would sense her anxiety, but if he did he chose not to bring it up. Knowing Harim's hatred for Romans, they didn't say a word to him about their fear. But then Harim never told them that he had been meeting his friends at their secret rendezvous spot.

This time Harim made a point of getting there early. When Imlah, who had given Harim a hard time for being late the last time, arrived later Harim waved at him with a large, mocking grin. Imlah glowered at him and sat down on the ground as far away from Harim as possible.

"I just heard that over fifty soldiers were killed when they were escorting a caravan on the way to Magdala,"

Zedekiah said, smiling. "That's because a band of our brothers were organized. They won a real battle just like I have been saying would be possible."

"Just the same, evidently another one of our friends decided he had waited long enough to get organized," Gedaliah said, "and took it upon himself to kill one of those Roman scum and dump him into the sea."

After the other Zealots finished cheering, Zedekiah raised his hands, his face red with rage. "You fools!" he shouted. "If it were not for Harim and his father the Romans would have produced a blood bath. The soldiers searched the hills looking for those that attacked the caravan. They failed but didn't take it out on our people. Yet, they would never allow one of their men to be *murdered* without eventually arresting some Jew for killing him. Are you so stupid that you don't see the difference?"

Harim felt embarrassed by this high praise from Zedekiah. He had opposed his father's going to report finding the body. Besides, his father was the one that had explained why a Jew couldn't have been the killer while he stood mute.

"Tell us, Harim, what exactly happened when you talked with the Roman captain?" Zedekiah asked.

The last thing Harim wanted to do was give them the impression that he had softened in his hatred for the Romans. "The captain questioned us about where we found the body and how we knew he had been murdered. My father said that we found it near our boat, and that he had been stabbed in the back. When the captain accused us of having killed him, my father pointed out that he must have been murdered on the Sabbath during which Jews didn't stray from home on that day."

"It sounds to me like you were favorably impressed by their captain," Gedaliah mocked sourly. "Maybe you should join them as a spy or a tax collector."

Harim jumped to his feet and made a lunge at Gedaliah, but was restrained by two other men. "Say that again,

Gedaliah, and it will be the last thing you'll ever say! I only told the truth as to what happened, which is something you're incapable of doing. I never said that I *liked* the captain."

Gedaliah took several steps toward Harim but was grabbed by the arm by a large, powerful man. "Take one more step or say another word Gedaliah, and I'll have Simon break your arm!" Zedekiah growled. "I didn't ask Harim what happened because I was being nosy but because I want to know how their captain thinks. Something you obviously have a hard time doing. So either shut-up or you can go have a talk with the Roman captain to see what *you* can learn."

The men restraining Harim and Gedaliah slowly released them, and they stood still. Zedekiah looked at Harim. "What else can you tell me about the captain, Harim?"

"You said you want to know how he thinks. He's certainly no one's fool. I think he's intelligent and devious. From what I could tell, his men either fear him or respect him. He did treat us fairly." Harim then guessed, without any reason other than his hatred, "I think he's very ruthless and would never show any mercy."

"Some patriot you are," Gedaliah mumbled sarcastically. "You state with absolute *certainty* that he's fair and intelligent, but only *think* that he is ruthless and would show no mercy. I never met him but I can tell you with out a doubt that he's ruthless and merciless, just like all Romans."

Zephaniah stood. "It seems that no one else here has heard that the Romans had found out where a large number of Zealots were camped. They were the ones who had attacked the caravan. Two hundred were killed. The men you saw crucified along the road into Capernaum were all that were left."

Everyone stared at Zephaniah in stunned disbelief. No one knew what to say. Finally, Zedekiah said, "I'll let you know when we'll meet again."

*   *   *

Meanwhile, Captain Drusus enjoyed his meal of radishes and onions thinly sliced into fish broth, along with bread and wine. Sergeant Lucius came in and interrupted his meal. "There is a woman outside who insists she has information about the soldier who was murdered."

"Is she a Jew?"

"No, she is a Roman. By the looks of her I'd say that she is very wealthy."

Drusus wiped his mouth with his sleeve. "Well, well. Who knows, she just might be able to help us. Bring her in, Lucius."

A tall, skinny woman in her early forties followed Lucius into Drusus' quarters, sniffing the foul smelling air. She was dressed in a colorful Roman outfit with an exquisite necklace of rubies, emeralds and sapphires around her thin neck. Her face was heavily made up, and Drusus silently assumed that she was trying to hide her wrinkles.

"My Sergeant tells me that you have information about the soldier who was found murdered," Drusus said.

"I know all there is to know," she replied, her voice pitched high, her tone condescending. "My name is Marian and my husband is Phasaelus. He owns most of the ships that comes from Macedonia. My husband is the murderer! He killed Patrobas because he suspected that I was having an affair with him."

Drusus didn't care if she was actually having an affair or not but knew that arresting such an influential Roman for murder could pose political problems. "Why have you waited so long to report all this?"

"Because my husband had bribed Patrobas' captain to tell me that Patrobas had been transferred to Judea. Tertius Rufus, who was a good friend of Patrobas, only told me earlier this morning what really happened."

If Marian wanted to rid herself of her husband blaming him for murder would be a good way to do it, Drusus thought. "Who was your husband's captain?"

"Titus Phineas."

Drusus knew he could verify her story by checking with Tertius Rufus later inasmuch as he was under his command. "Where is your husband now?"

"He's home talking with a ship builder about building another ship. We live in the large estate on top of the hill next to the home of Gaius Maximus."

Drusus looked at Lucius. "Take two of your men to arrest Phasaelus." Then he looked at Marian. "Thank you for coming to tell me this."

Lucius followed her out the door and went to get his two men. Drusus got up to watch them walk away. Then Drusus motioned for a soldier to come to him. "Find Tertius Rufus and tell him that I want to see him at once. If she's lying Phasaelus could make life miserable for me."

It wasn't very long before a young, husky man appeared in the doorway. "You wanted to see me, Captain?" he asked nervously.

"I understand that you told Marian that her husband killed Patrobas," Drusus barked, glaring at Rufus. "Is that true?"

"Yes, sir."

"Why the devil didn't you tell me about it?"

"I didn't want to get Phineas in trouble. I had no idea Marian would come tell you."

"You're a fool. You knew we've been searching for the killer. Are you sure that her husband killed him?"

"Yes. Patrobas told me several days earlier that Phasaelus had threatened to kill him. Patrobas also had said that Phineas had warned him that his life in danger. But once Patrobas was dead, Phasaelus paid Phineas to tell Marian that Patrobas had been transferred."

Drusus banged his hand on the table. "I'll have Phineas' hide for concealing a murder!" Rufus held his breath in anticipation of being punished. "That's all, Rufus," Drusus said. "Now get out of here before I have you whipped."

Not much later Lucius and two soldiers banged on the door of Phasaelus' large, extravagant house. Double rows of Ionic columns supported a balcony that went around the entire house. When a servant opened the door, Lucius pushed his way passed him.

"We're here to arrest Phasaelus for the murder of Patrobas," Lucius said. "Where is he?"

"My master's out in the terrace in the back of the house talking with his ship builder."

"Take us there."

The servant led them through the banquet room with its reclining sofas that encircled a long oak table. Ornamented woodcarvings formed a crown molding on all the walls. The servant stopped at the wide archway that opened up to the courtyard. A marble fountain sprayed a faint mist into the air. An assortment of pomegranate, palm and sycamore trees provided needed shade from the hot sun.

Two men sat at a marble table under one of the sycamore trees studying a drawing of a ship. They looked up in alarm at Lucius and his two soldiers. "Which one of you is Phasaelus?" Lucius asked.

A short, chubby man in his fifties with graying hair and bushy beard slowly stood up. "I'm Phasaelus, and this is Lehabim, my master shipbuilder. What do you want?"

"I came to arrest you for the murder of Patrobas," Lucius answered, motioning his men to grab Phasaelus. "Take him!"

Phasaelus lowered his head and held out his arms to the soldiers in submission. He neither resisted physically nor insisted that he was innocent. His guilt was written over his defeated face as clearly as a written confession.

As a Roman citizen Phasaelus was permitted to have a lawyer help him, but he was still found guilt of killing Patrobas. Rome crucified non-Romans for insurrection but seldom crucified Roman citizens. Phasaelus' wife smiled as she watched him being hanged for the murder of Patrobas.

*   *   *

Suddenly and unexpectedly the soldiers stopped questioning the residents of Capernaum. Not being aware of Phasaelus' trial and execution, the Jews had no idea that the crime had been solved. Baffled by the cessation of the investigation, they were just as jittery and afraid as they had been.

Two days after the questioning had stopped, Captain Drusus, accompanied by two soldiers, went to Elhanan's home. When Sarah opened the door and saw him she assumed the worst. Her knees buckled in terror, thinking, *My God, they have come to arrest my husband.*

Drusus caught her before she fell to the floor. "Easy there, woman! I'm not here to arrest your husband. I'm Captain Drusus, the man your husband had reported the murder of one of my men to. I came to tell him that we found our killer." He released her. "Is he at home?"

Sarah, having no way of knowing if he was telling the truth, was thankful Elhanan wasn't home. She braced herself against the edge of the doorway. "No, he's fishing with our two sons."

"That's too bad. Your husband is a remarkable man and I wanted to thank him again for having the courage to come talk with me. When he gets home tell him that Captain Marcus Drusus wanted him to know that his insistence that a Jew didn't commit the murder was correct. The killer turned out to be Roman, and a wealthy one at that. The man murdered what he believed was his wife's lover."

"I'll tell him as soon as he gets home," Sarah replied.

"Good. Oh, and your husband might find it interesting that it was the killer's wife who turned him in. Apparently she loved the dead man more than she did her husband after all."

Sarah stood in the doorway in relief as she watched them walk away. She then spied Rachel hurrying up the road toward home. Rachel, who had seen the soldiers leaving her house, feared the same horrible motive for their presence that her mother had. Even from a distance Sarah could tell from the terrified expression on her daughter's face what she was thinking.

Before Rachel could say anything upon reaching her mother, Sarah took her hands in hers. "It's all right, Rachel! They came to tell your father that they caught the killer."

Rachel sighed and hugged her mother. "Praise God for His mercy. I was terrified when I saw them."

As they went into the house Rachel realized that one of the two soldiers she had passed in her haste toward home had been her unknown protector. She turned and looked down the road but the soldiers were gone.

When Elhanan, Harim and Gideon arrived home Sarah said, "You won't believed what happened, Elhanan."

"By the expression on your face it must have been something good," Elhanan replied.

"A captain by the name of Marcus Drusus and two other soldiers came here to tell you that they found the killer."

"Thank the Almighty," Elhanan said, sighing. "I was starting to wonder if they would ever find the killer. Did Drusus say anything else?"

"Yes. He wanted to thank you for reporting that you had found the body. I must admit that I was terrified when they came here. I was sure they were going to arrest you."

Elhanan noticed Harim glance at his mother in amazement. "I'm glad that's over," Elhanan said. "That explains why the soldiers stopped questioning everyone. We'll have to tell our neighbors to spread the word so they won't be worried anymore. I'm surprised Captain Drusus bothered to come to tell me."

Jehoram asked in his high-pitched voice, "How was fishing today, Father?"

"About average, Jehoram," Elhanan answered, reaching out to mess up Jehoram's black hair.

Rachel and Harim ate their meal in silence, contemplating a different matter altogether. For Rachel, it was her infatuation for one particular unknown Roman soldier with kind eyes. For Harim, it was his hatred for all Romans.

Chapter Six

The following day was the Sabbath, and arrived with its typical religious observances. When it was over at dusk Rachel helped her mother clear away the table. Then Rachel went outside and sat on a wood bench. She looked up at the bright stars twinkling in the cloudless sky. A slight breeze brought welcome relief from the intense heat of the sun that had been so oppressive during the day.

Rachel closed her eyes as she tilted her head toward the sky thinking how she might find out who was the Roman with the blue eyes. *Going to the garrison to ask Captain Drusus is out of the question. A Jewish woman can't possibly go there.* She felt frustrated by what seemed a hopeless prospect.

Gideon came out of the house and sat down next to her. He looked at Rachel. "Wasn't it fantastic to hear that they solved the murder of that Roman soldier? Now our friends and neighbors won't have to be afraid of being arrested."

Rachel smiled at him, putting her arm around his shoulder. "Yes, it was wonderful, Gideon, but Harim didn't seem very happy about it though. I imagine his resentment for the Romans clouded his appreciation for what Captain Drusus did by coming here to tell father . . ."

She stopped when suddenly an idea popped into her head. She looked at Gideon, wondering if it was wise to enlist his help. Her mind was torn between her desire to find out the name of her protector and the problems it would cause if her family found out about it. She leaned toward Gideon to whisper, "Gideon, I wonder if you would do me a great favor, but you must *never* tell anyone about it?"

He looked at her in surprise. "You know that I would do anything for you Rachel, but why such secrecy?"

She gave a quick peek at the door to see if anyone might overhear them. "I'd like you to go the garrison, tell them who our father is and then ask to see Captain Drusus." She gave another furtive glance at the door. "He'll remember father. He came here yesterday to tell father that they caught the man who killed the soldier. Ask Captain Drusus the name of the soldier who has blue eyes who came to our house with him."

"Why do you want to know that?"

"Because the soldier had once helped me and I want to thank him."

"When did a soldier help you?"

"Several months ago. Will you do it for me?"

The excitement of going to the garrison outweighed any concern of potential risk he might have felt. "Of course I will," he replied without asking about how or why the soldier had helped her.

Rachel kissed him on the cheek. "Remember, Gideon, you must not tell anyone what I asked you to do. Father and mother would be very angry with both of us. Me for asking you to go to the garrison, and you for going."

Gideon waited nine days before he had the chance to keep his promise to Rachel. His father sprained his ankle and could barely walk. Gideon felt sorry about his father's ankle, but was happy he could finally keep his word to Rachel.

After they finished breakfast, Elhanan looked at Harim and Gideon. "We won't be going fishing today. You two can do what you want, but only after you've finished your chores."

Harim scraped the bottom of their boat to remove the barnacles while Gideon picked corn from their small cornfield. Gideon carried a sack of corn and dropped it inside the door. He looked his father. "I'm going now, if that's all right."

Elhanan nodded, and Gideon walked out of the house. Rachel's face flushed with anxiety as she watched her younger brother slowly walk out of the house and then race down the road. She knew precisely where he was headed. Gideon hadn't mentioned to Rachel that he had decided to include two of his friends in his adventure.

Gideon stopped at Elizabad's, and then Ishbak's house to ask them to come with him. His invitation to each of them was word-for-word identical. "I'm going to the garrison to talk with the Roman captain," he said excitedly. "Come with me."

Their responses differed only slightly. Elizabad asked in alarm, "Are you crazy, Gideon? The captain at the garrison wouldn't want to talk with you."

"Yes he will. He knows my father." After Gideon coaxed him with promises of how thrilling it would be, Elizabad agreed to go.

Later when he invited Ishbak, his friend said, "You're both out of your mind! A Roman captain would never waste his time talking with you."

Gideon used the same irresistible bait he had used on Elizabad to entice him to agree to go. Ishbak accepted as well. The three friends skipped along the road in carefree spirits until they came within ten yards of the garrison. They saw two muscular soldiers guarding the large open gate to the garrison. They stopped dead in their tracks and watched one soldier sharpening the shiny, sleek blade of his sword with a whetstone.

"I changed my mind," Elizabad said in a quiet voice. "I'll wait here until you come out."

Gideon and Ishbak each took an arm to pulled Elizabad up to the gate. The soldier glared at them. "Where do you three brats think you're going? This isn't a place for children to play. Get out of here before I crack you over the head!"

This time *both* Elizabad and Ishbak wanted to leave, but Gideon made a promise he was determined to keep. "I want to ask Captain Drusus a question, sir," he replied more bravely than he felt.

The soldier was surprised that a Jewish boy knew the name of his captain. The thought occurred to him that if the boy knew his captain's name, perhaps Drusus knew him as well. "What do you want to ask him?"

Gideon wasn't sure if his promise to Rachel not to tell anyone applied to a Roman soldier or only to his family. He realized that if he *didn't* answer the soldier's question he certainly wouldn't have the chance to talk with Captain Drusus. "I need to ask him the name of a soldier who helped my sister some time ago," he answered, clearing his dry throat. "My sister wants to thank him."

"What makes you think my captain can tell you his name?"

"My sister said that the soldier she wants to thank came to our house recently with Captain Drusus. He came to thank my father for reporting the death of a soldier."

Is it possible that Captain Drusus went to a Jew's house to thank him for something? the guard wondered. *Surely he would have summoned a Jew to come to him.* These were precarious waters and the soldier decided to play it safe. "Follow me," he said less harshly.

When they reached Drusus' quarters the soldier knocked on the open door. "Excuse me, Captain, but there's a Jewish boy here who claims that you went to his house recently. He said he wants to ask you a question."

Drusus looked up at the soldier. "What the devil are you talking about? When did I go to . . . wait a minute, I remember now. About two weeks ago I went to thank Elhanan for telling us about Patrobas. Bring him in."

The soldier stepped aside and all three youngsters walked in. They stopped and stood nervously less than two feet from the open door. Drusus rose, walked toward them and studied their faces. "I recall that Elhanan had his son with him but none of you resemble him at all."

Gideon said with a dry mouth, "That was my older brother, Harim. I'm Gideon, his second son."

Drusus gave a slight smile. "That's right, his name was Harim. Your father did say that he had two other sons and a daughter." He walked back to his chair, sat down, leaned back and folded his arms. "What did you want to ask me?"

"When you came to our house recently there were two other soldiers with you. My sister said one had blue eyes. She told me he helped her sometime ago. She wanted to thank him but doesn't know his name. She wanted me to ask you for his name."

Drusus laughed. "She noticed his blue eyes, did she? That was Sergeant Lucius, my second in command. Did you want to talk with him?"

"No sir, I just wanted his name for my sister," Gideon answered, much to the relief of Elizabad and Ishbak. "Thank you very much, sir."

"It was my pleasure, Gideon. Give my regards to your father. I admire his courage. It seems that you have inherited it."

The three friends turned and ran out of the strange world of military power. "If you ever want to go to the garrison again, Gideon, count me out," Elizabad said. "I don't want to go through that again."

*　　*　　*

Hatred, like all strong emotions, devours those who are obsessed by it day after day, month after month, ad infinitum. Such was the case for Gedaliah, the man who had argued with Harim so spitefully. When he was twelve-years-old he had witnessed the crucifixion of three Jews who were accused of robbing a tax collector, and never forgot it. Now at twenty-three, he was a bitter man whose every thought was about killing Romans.

Gedaliah had once said, "You either killed Romans or you were their friend. When it comes to dealing with Roman soldiers, there's no such thing as moderation."

Harim was surprised to see Gedaliah waiting for him at the dock when he, his father and Gideon came home from fishing. While they unloaded the catch for the day from the boat, Gedaliah said, "When you're done, Harim, I'd like to talk with you for a minute."

After they finished putting the fish on a cart, Harim and Gedaliah walked together down the road toward Harim's home. Gideon walked with his father who pushed the cartload of fish about twenty yards in front of them. Harim was thirsty, hot, exhausted and not in the mood for another argument. "What do want to talk with me about, Gedaliah?"

Gedaliah answered softly so he wouldn't be overheard. "I've been thinking about when Zedekiah asked about your visit to the garrison. He failed to ask you the most important question."

"What question was that?"

"When you walked through the garrison, did you happen to notice if there were any vulnerable spots along the top of the wall?"

"What do mean? Vulnerable in what way?"

"Don't be so stupid, Harim. You know precisely what I mean! Places where soldiers were not posted. Gaps in the walkways along the top of the wall where there were no guards. Places where steps lead down inside the courtyard, or a building screens their view from seeing what's around the bend."

Harim stopped walking and turned toward Gedaliah. "If you're thinking what I think you are, Gedaliah, you must be crazy. There are over six thousand soldiers in the garrison." Gedaliah glared at Harim. "Don't tell *me* how many soldiers there are!" He had raised his voice more than he had intended, and noticed Elhanan glance back at them. He lowered his voice, and asked, "Were there any vulnerable spots, or not?"

"Not that I noticed, no. Certainly none that could be attacked without our being seen and getting slaughtered."

"I'm not suggesting an all out attack during the day, you fool. I'm thinking about a small group of us sneaking up and ambushing a few of the soldiers on top of the wall. From there we could shoot flaming arrows on top of their barracks while the soldiers are sleeping. We could escape before they knew what hit them."

Harim didn't say anything, thinking seriously about Gedaliah's scheme. After a few moments, Harim replied, "Forget it! Even if there were such a gap along the wall, which there *isn't*, the other soldiers on top of the wall would either hear or see us before we ever had time to light the arrows."

"It sounds to me like you have been taken in by Zedekiah's idea to wait to build an army while our brothers are being murdered. Or did you forget what Zephaniah told us about the Zealots who were slaughtered?"

"My memory is as good as yours," Harim answered. "What's your point?"

"Just what it was when I said that we must kill Romans whenever we can. Are you sure you aren't going soft in your feelings toward Rome since your friendly visit with their captain?"

Harim grabbed his arm and spun him around to face him. "I warned you before about accusing me of that," he snarled, pulling out his knife and putting it under Gedaliah's chin. "Say it again, and you won't have the chance to kill anyone."

Gedaliah grinned mockingly. "Put your knife away boy before I take it from you and stick it in your gut. I don't need your help. Try using your knife on a Roman sometime."

Harim lowered his knife, and they walked away from each other without saying another word. After taking a few steps, Harim turned to watch Gedaliah walking down the road. He resented Gedaliah's accusation but was confused by his mixed feelings. His father thought he hated the Romans *too* much, and his so-called friend thought he didn't hate them enough. He was beginning to question exactly how he *did* feel.

Harim resumed walking home, aware that when he arrived his father would undoubtedly question him about his heated discussion with Gedaliah. Elhanan was chopping wood when he saw Harim coming.

"I want to talk with you for a minute, Harim," he called out, wiping the sweat pouring off his forehead. Harim took a few steps toward his father as Elhanan resumed cutting wood. "I couldn't help but overhear your friend say something about how many soldiers that were in the garrison. What was that all about?"

"Oh, he was only asking about how many soldiers were there when we were questioned by Captain Drusus. He didn't believe me when I told him there were only two. He insisted that their captain would never have questioned us without having more soldiers with him to intimidate us."

Harim took the axe from his father as Elhanan replied, "Your friend seemed very angry to have disagreed over such a trivial thing. Who was this friend of yours?"

"Gedaliah, but I don't think you ever met him," Harim answered, avoiding looking his father in the eyes as he chopped the wood. "He's more of an acquaintance than actually a friend. I barely know him."

"That's enough wood for now, Harim." When Harim put down the axe, Elhanan took him by the arm and stared into his eyes. "I trust that this acquaintance of yours is *not* a Zealot. You know how your mother and I feel about your getting involved with them"

*   *   *

By this time the followers of Jesus had witnessed him perform dozens of astonishing miracles. Understandably, the size of the crowds had grown larger and larger. Some people were merely curious but many others were seeking healing. As they strolled together from place to place Jesus taught them about the Kingdom of God.

Such was the case when a leper fell on his knees before Jesus. He looked up at Jesus and said, "Jesus, if you are willing, I know you can make me clean."

Jesus looked deep into the man's sad eyes, reached out and touched him. Phillip, afraid that Jesus would be infected, was about to protest but Jesus spoke first. "Be clean! Your faith has healed you."

The man rose from his knees with tears in his eyes. He looked at Jesus and said, "Thank you, Lord. May I go with you?"

Jesus smiled and put his hand on the man's shoulder. "No. I want you to go home and tell your family the good news."

The ex-leper walked away singing praises to God for His mercy. Although the disciples of Jesus were thrilled by what Jesus did they were no longer surprised. As Jesus and his followers continued walking, Phillip whispered his concern to Andrew. "Jesus has healed other people without touching them. Why did he touch the leper this time? Not only did he risk being infected with the contagion, he also broke the commandment about not touching a person who is unclean."

"Why ask me?" Andrew whispered. "If you have a problem with what Jesus did why not ask him? All I know is that the man was cleansed."

"I know that. I just don't know why Jesus touched him when he healed others by just saying the words. It's as if Jesus at times seems to go out of His way to upset our religious leaders who insist that we obey the laws handed down to us for centuries."

Over the next several months, the disciples saw Jesus repeatedly touching those considered unclean. One day Phillip asked Jesus, "Master, why do you touch people who are unclean? You've touched a woman with an issue of blood, a dead body, lepers and even Gentiles."

Jesus smiled at Phillip. "I'll ask you a question, Phillip. According to our ancient teaching what happens when the spiritually *clean* touches the *unclean?*"

"That which had been clean becomes unclean."

"You're right, Phillip. That's what the law says. Yet, God looks at the heart, not the body. The law was made for man, not man for the law. The law will not forgive nor cleanse. I do both. That's why when I touch the unclean they become *clean.*"

"I understand now, Lord," Phillip said.

Chapter Seven

Drusus and Lucius were in the stable looking at a new Arabian horse Lucius gave Drusus to replace his horse that died. Drusus stroked the horse neck. "It's a fine horse, Lucius. Thank you. Where did you get it?"

"From a Sheik who arrived in Capernaum yesterday. He's selling twenty horses and I couldn't resist this one. I knew you'd like him."

"I do, indeed. You always were a good judge of horses."

"The Sheik had sold five horses to Herod in Jerusalem and came here on his way to Hazor. That reminds me, the Sheik told me when he was in Jerusalem there was quite a stir. Your good friend Herod had John the Baptist executed."

They both laughed when Lucius called Herod his friend. "You were right when you said his wife Herodias would be behind it," Lucius said. "According to the Sheik, Herod was content to let him rot in prison, but Herodias tricked him into having the prophet beheaded."

"How did she manage that?"

"It happened when Herod gave an elaborate party to impress his friends. Herod told Herodias' daughter, Salome, he'd give her anything she wanted if she danced for them. When she finished dancing she asked for John the Baptist's head on a platter."

"She sounds . . . like her . . . mother," Drusus said, noticing a man walking toward his quarters. He swung his leg over the horse's head and jumped off. "Come with me, Lucius. There's a man I hope has news for us."

When they caught up to the man Drusus took him by the arm. "Let's go inside so we can talk in private."

The three of them entered Drusus' quarters. "Close the door, Lucius," Drusus said as he looked at the seer. "Well, what did you find out?" The seer glanced at Lucius. "Don't worry about him," Drusus said, "you can talk freely in front of him. This is my second in command, Sergeant Lucius."

"At least five hundred Zealots are meeting near Chorazin tomorrow night," the seer said. "I can't tell you how to get to where they're meeting but I can take you there."

"Good, that's less than five miles from here," Drusus replied. "Lucius, I want you to take two thousand men with you and follow this man to the Zealots' meeting place. Bring back as many prisoners as possible."

Lucius stared at the seer but didn't say anything. *He looks like a Jew,* he thought. *Why is he betraying his own people?*

*   *   *

Harim hadn't forgotten his promise to Gideon to find out all that he could about Jesus. After returning from fishing and having supper he went to see an old friend of the family, Simri Ben Ruhamah. "Hello, Simri," Harim said, "you're looking well."

"Looks are deceiving, my young friend. I feel like I'm ready to join my fathers in heaven. I haven't seen you for a long time. How your family?"

"Mother and father are fine, I'm happy to say. So are my brothers and sister. I suppose you're wondering why I came."

"The thought did occur to me but I knew you'd get around to telling me. I assumed it wasn't to ask about my health."

"No, I'm embarrassed to admit, it wasn't. I promised Gideon that I would talk with several knowledgeable people about a particular rabbi called Jesus. Gideon thinks he might be the Messiah. Do you know anything about him?"

"I can't say that I *know* anything from personal experience, but I've heard about him. However, I learned long ago not to believe everything I hear. I suggest you do the same."

"What have you heard?"

"I heard that he preaches about the coming of God's Kingdom, forgiving our enemies and repentance. I also heard he has broken the Sabbath, eats with tax collectors and performs miracles."

"The Messiah is supposed to deliver us from our Roman oppressors, not forgive them. This Jesus sounds like a coward to me. Besides, breaking the Sabbath and eating with tax collectors proves this man isn't the Messiah. Thank you, Simri, you confirmed my suspicion."

"Don't be too hasty to pass judgment on anyone, Harim. I've lived long enough to know we seldom know enough to condemn someone else. I only told you about various rumors that I've heard. I suggest you talk with people who have seen and heard Jesus themselves, not just rumors about him."

"I intend to talk with Nahum," Harim replied. "Thanks for your advice."

"I'd like to give you one more piece of advice. I could tell how much you hate the Romans from your reaction when I mentioned Jesus teaches forgiveness. Temper your passion with mercy and justice. Hating all Romans is no better than the Romans hating all Jews." Simri smiled and added, "Tell your parents I said, 'Shalom'."

"I will."

Harim went to Nahum's house. Nahum sat at his desk writing out a contract for two men. Nahum was a well-known scribe who wrote important papers for those who couldn't write. He was a short, heavyset man in his earlier sixties with gray hair and long, gray beard. He motioned for Harim to sit down and wait until he finished.

After the two men were gone Nahum said, "What are you doing here, Harim? I know your father can read and write."

"I'm not here to ask you to write anything, Nahum. I came to ask you about someone for Gideon. Do you know anything about the Rabbi they call Jesus?"

"Listen Harim, you don't want to get involved with that trouble-maker. Jesus and his followers have deluded many of our people into thinking he is the Messiah. They have broken the Sabbath numerous times by picking wheat and prepared a meal on the Sabbath. Worse, Jesus healed a man on the Sabbath and committed blasphemy by proclaiming he did so by the power of God."

"That's what my father already told Gideon, but you know Gideon. He has some foolish idea that this man could heal Jehoram."

Nahum leaned back and rubbed his stiff writing hand. "You must tell Gideon to stay away from Jesus if he knows what's good for him. Jesus plays upon peoples' emotions by having people pretend to be healed to attract followers. Although on one occasion he apparently did cast out an evil spirit from a man who witnesses swore was possessed. Fortunately, a Pharisee was present and pointed out Jesus did so by the power of Satan. This fraud has been denounced publicly several times by our religious leaders for blasphemy, but his followers always manage to get him away before he could be arrested."

Harim stood up. "That's what I thought. Thank you for your help, Nahum. I'll tell Gideon what you told me about Jesus."

Harim left to go tell Gideon what he had learned. He knew Gideon would be deeply disappointed but thought it would be better if he knew the truth, not place his hope in such an evil man. When Harim arrived home Gideon was sitting in the shade of a cedar tree munching on an apple. Elhanan and Sarah sat on a bench outside their front door, twenty feet away.

Harim smiled at his parents. "Where's Jehoram?" he asked.

"He's in the house working on his temple," Sarah answered.

Harim walked over to Gideon. "Let's go for a walk, Gideon," Harim said loud enough for his parents to hear. "I want to show you a snake I just killed."

Gideon jumped up. "What kind of snake?"

"A cobra," Harim answered. They walked about a hundred yards when Harim said, "I didn't kill a snake, Gideon. The reason why I asked you to go for a walk was so I can tell you what I learned about the new rabbi."

Harim noticed Gideon's face light up in eager anticipation. Harim put his hand on his younger brother's shoulder, stopped walking and looked at Gideon. "I'm sorry, Gideon, but father was right to forbid you from getting your hopes up over this false rabbi. Both Simri and Nahum told me that Jesus has *tricked* people into thinking he can heal people. He's even broken the Sabbath. What's more, our religious leaders have denounced him for casting out an evil spirit by the power of Satan."

Gideon didn't say anything, but Harim could tell how disillusioned he felt. Harim knelt down in front of him and looked into his teary eyes. "I know how much you want Jehoram to be healed, Gideon. We all do, but Jesus is nothing more than a evil blasphemer."

Gideon sighed. "I should have know father was right when he told me about Jesus. Thank you for finding out about him for me, Harim." He tried to smile. "Don't worry about me, I'll get over it."

*   *   *

Fishing was always hard work. It was also unpredictable. They caught few fish, causing Elhanan to say, "Some days the fish are so plentiful it seems as if they're anxious to be caught, but not today. Today the Sea of Galilee resembles the *Dead Sea,* totally devoid of life. No matter where we cast our net it returns empty."

The hot sun beat down on Elhanan and his sons as they tried again and again to catch some fish, but to no avail. The calm water reflected the sun in their faces and the still air made it seem even hotter. Elhanan was disappointed, but he had experienced such days before and knew that he would again in the future.

He stretched his sore back. "That's it for today. Tomorrow is another day when we can try again. Let's head for home. Your mother will glad to see us even though we'll be coming home empty-handed."

Harim and Gideon shared their father's disappointment about going home with so little fish, but were happy at the prospect of arriving home earlier than usual. *I'll finally have the change to talk with Rachel about my visit to the garrison,* Gideon thought.

Good, Harim thought. *I didn't think I could make it but I'll be able to meet my friends after all.*

When they reached shore Harim asked, "Can I stay here to wait for the other boats to dock? I want to see if Ezra and his father get back in time to visit Nahash. He's building a new house now that his burned down."

"Fine," Elhanan answered, "but make sure you're home before supper."

As soon as Elhanan and Gideon were out of sight Harim ran to where he knew the Zealots were meeting. When he got there he was surprised to see over twenty new faces along with fifty familiar faces. They all sat on the ground scattered in a large circle. A lively discussion was already underway, and Harim sat down next to a sycamore tree to listen.

Some of the new men seemed willing to join the Zealots, but others were hesitant to become an active participant in a resistance movement. "I despise what the Romans do," one man said, "but I'm afraid that an all out rebellion against Rome will only lead to more crucifixions. I heard that two hundred men who we slaughtered recently. Frankly, I'm worried about what they might do to my family if we get caught."

Zedekiah rose to speak. His voice passionate, his eyes filled with hate. "You are afraid of what Rome *might* do, Jeremiah, but what about what they already *are* doing? Our families and friends are taken out of their homes without the slightest provocation. Some are sold into slavery and others are thrown into prison or killed. Is life under such cruel bondage worth the price of doing nothing? Is that really what you want to protect?"

A number of the men shouted angrily, "Never! Never!'

When the yelling stopped, Jeremiah said, "I want freedom as much as any of you but not to see my family and friends slaughtered. There are over thirty thousand trained soldiers in Galilee. How can a handful of Jews fight them?"

"That's exactly what I have been saying all along!" Zedekiah answered. "You're new here, but those have been with me from the beginning will tell you that." He walked around, looking different men in the eyes. "Even a handful of two hundred can't fight them and *win*. That's why I have been insisting that we must build an army to fight an army. There are tens of thousands of men just like us who long to be free. We can put together an army of over a hundred thousand if we try. The only thing stopping us is our own timid unwillingness to try."

This time the enthusiastic cheers were such that no one risked arguing. Zedekiah raised both hands in the air. "There are many groups of Zealots throughout Galilee already, but they're not organized into a single force. I need you to find out where they are and tell them that I intend to build an army. It will take time, but it can and will be done! Ask their leaders to meet with us here in thirty days. Then we'll know how many men we already have and how much work we have to do to build an army."

A new recruit stood up. "I'm Hariph. My brother, Conaniah, had been part of the two hundred Zealots who were ambushed by the Romans. Most were slaughtered, but he and seven others survived. What did the Romans do with the prisoners? They were the eight men who were crucified along the road leading out of Capernaum, that's what! They and my brother died for our freedom. They also proved Zedekiah is right. Two hundred men were not enough. We need an army."

"We'll meet here in thirty days," Zedekiah said. "Let's build our army!"

*   *   *

Meanwhile Lucius and his men followed the seer in plenty of time to get to Chorazin before dark. "It's only about half a mile from here," the seer told Lucius.

Lucius looked at his second in command. "Tell the men we'll rest here for a while. I don't want them exhausted and thirsty when we attack." He looked at the seer. "Where exactly are the Zealots?"

"They meet in a large cave on the other side of that hill."

Lucius didn't know who this man was or how he knew so much but he didn't trust him. Thirty minutes later, Lucius said, "Gnaeus, tell the men it's time to move out."

Just before they arrived at the cave Lucius summoned three of his subordinates. "We're almost there. This is what we'll do. Half of our men will attack straight ahead. Pileha and I will lead them. I want the other half to form half a circle and move forward to stop any from escaping. Shedeur, you and Parosh are in charge of them. Drive them into the cave if possible."

When they were ready Lucius lead the charge. The Zealots, taken completely by surprise, scattered in disarray without bothering to pick up their shields. Dozens fled into the cave, many others tried to run but most fought where they stood. No one surrendered. The battle was short and bloody. The soldiers, protected by their shields, lost seven men with another thirteen wounded. A large number of the wounded Zealots took their own lives, rather than face crucifixion. It took almost as long to go through the men to gather up the wounded soldiers and wounded Zealots as the battle itself.

Pileha said, "There are eighteen rebels still alive, Sergeant Lucius. What do you want to do with them?"

Lucius, remembering the last time he brought wounded men to Capernaum, answered, "Bring them here." He looked at the seer standing behind him. He had tears in his eyes. *I wonder what that's all about?* Lucius thought. The wounded were brought to Lucius. They were young, bloody and frightened.

"You men realize that I can take you to Capernaum to be crucified," Lucius said. "I want you to raise your hand, tell me your name and swear by the name of your God that you'll never fight against Rome again." He walked to each of them, stared them in the eyes and said, "Swear!"

One by one they raised their hand, gave their name and said, "I promise in Jehovah's Holy Name never to fight against Rome again."

Lucius looked at Pileha. "I want you and five of our men to stay here, bind their wounds and then let them go. I'll leave six horses for you to catch up with us." He held up his hand and yelled, "The rest of you follow me back to Capernaum."

* * *

97

When Elhanan and Gideon arrived home Rachel wasn't there. The aroma of freshly baked bread made Gideon's mouth water. Sarah, noticing him staring at the bread, sliced off a large piece and handed it to him. "No more, Gideon, until supper." She looked at Elhanan. "Where's Harim?"

"He went to see how Nahash is coming along on his house. I'm afraid we didn't catch much fish today. Hopefully we'll do better tomorrow."

"Where's Rachel?" Gideon asked his mother.

"She went to get water from the well down the street."

"I'll go help her carry it," Gideon said, charging out the door and down the road before Sarah or Elhanan could say a word.

"There's a change for you," Elhanan said, smiling at Sarah. "I never knew Gideon to be anxious to help Rachel with her chores."

Rachel was headed home when Gideon met her. "I'll carry the water for you, Rachel."

"No thank you, Gideon. I can manage. Besides, what would your friends think if they saw you carrying a jug of water on your head like a woman?"

"I wanted to talk with you before you got home. I went to the garrison as I promised and found out the name you wanted."

She froze in her tracks and put the jug of water on the ground. "What's his name?"

"His name is Lucius. He's a sergeant."

"Sergeant Lucius," she said, putting the jug of water back on her head. "Who told you his name? Captain Drusus?"

"Yes, it was. Soldiers were everywhere. One almost forced us to leave before I had the chance to talk with Captain Drusus. The garrison sure is a scary place."

"What do you mean by *us*, Gideon? This was supposed to be our secret."

Gideon's face turned red. "I asked Ishbak and Elizabad to go with me, but I didn't tell them *why* we were going there."

Rachel wasn't happy he had taken two of his friends with him but what was done was done. "I appreciate that you went there and talked with their captain. I really do. But remember, not a word to anyone about this. Did Captain Drusus say anything else?"

"Not after I told him that Elhanan was our father."

*   *   *

Later that night Rachel lay in bed wondering what she could do now that she knew Lucius' name. She could no more go to the garrison now to talk with him anymore than she could have before. Rachel didn't want to ask Gideon to go back to the garrison, and asking Harim to go for her was out of the question. Unable to sleep, Rachel crept up on the roof to think in the cool night air. Everyone else in the family was asleep. She looked at the silhouette of the mountain range in the distance and the moon reflecting off the sea.

Rachel sighed deeply. *There must be some way to meet Lucius, but how?* She looked at the rooftops of the houses in her beloved city. Her eyes happened to fall on Martha's house. Martha's husband had said numerous times that he wished there was some way he could do something for her after she helped Martha so much. Rachel tried to dismiss the thought from her mind, hoping to come up with something else. But no matter hard she tried she couldn't purge from her mind the only idea she had. After struggling for sometime she decided to talk with Caleb.

*   *   *

The next morning Rachel tended to her chores faster than usual, her stomach churning and heart racing. When she finished all her duties, she said to her mother, "I'm going to Martha's now."

"Be sure to tell her that we are praying for her family. And give her my love."

"I will," Rachel said, walking out the door. Then she ran as fast as she could, hoping to catching Caleb before he left on his fishing boat. She saw him leaving the house on his way down the road toward the dock. "Caleb, wait a minute," she yelled, running toward him. "I'd like to ask a great favor of you."

Caleb stopped and turned to wait for her. "I'd be happy to do anything for you I can. Walk with me to my boat and tell me what is it?"

"Before you say that you will do it there are some things I need to tell you. For one thing, I want you to know that my parents would object strongly to my asking this of you if they knew about it. For another thing, I'm going to tell Martha about it. If she doesn't want you to do it then by all means you mustn't. Lastly, it might make things awkward for you if your friends knew what you did."

Caleb laughed. "Is that all? It sounds like you're trying to talk me out of it even before I know what the favor is. Now that I've been sufficiently warned, Rachel, what do you want me to do?"

"You probably heard that two soldiers came to our house recently. They came to tell my father they found out that a Roman had killed the man who was found dead near our boat."

"Yes, I heard about that. I imagine it had to be very frightening for your family when they knocked on your door. But what does that have to do with the favor you want of me?"

"One of the two soldiers with Captain Drusus was a sergeant called Lucius. I wasn't home when they came, and didn't see them until they were leaving. I want you to deliver a letter from me to Sergeant Lucius."

"You're going to write a letter to a Roman soldier," Caleb replied, grinning. "Rachel, I'd be happy to do anything for you after all that you've done for my family. It's none of my business, but why in the world do you want to write a letter to one of the soldiers who came to your house?"

"Some time before my father and my brother went to the garrison to report the dead soldier, Sergeant Lucius and two other soldiers stopped me in the street and asked me if I knew about a Zealot called Zedekiah. When I said I never heard of him one of the soldiers threatened to have me arrested. Sergeant Lucius ordered him to let me go. I was on my way to your house at the time. When I got to your house I told Martha all about it, but I only learned what his name is yesterday. I never had the chance to thank him and I want to thank him in my letter for what he did."

They reached Caleb's boat and stopped. "You write your letter, Rachel, and confer with my wife to get her sanction. If she approves, which I'm sure she will, I'll deliver your letter when I get back tonight." He reached and took her hand. "I'll make sure I get back from fishing in plenty of time."

Rachel watched him climb into his small fishing boat and adjust the single sail to catch the wind. As he sailed away she began to second-guess her plan. *What if Lucius doesn't remember me? What if my mother had been right and he's as cruel as any other soldier?*

Caleb was almost out of sight when she turned and started to walk toward Martha's house. *What will my parents do if they found out I asked Gideon to go to the garrison and Caleb to deliver my letter to Lucius? I won't be able to keep it a secret forever.*

Rachel was almost at Martha's when she stopped and looked at her house. She swallowed hard, walked up and knocked on Martha's door. Martha opened the door with a broad smile.

"Good morning, Rachel. I wasn't sure if you would be coming today when you hadn't shown up yet. Come in and sit down. The baby's still asleep." Martha noticed Rachel's gloomy expression. "Are you all right? You don't look very well."

Rachel sat down at the table. "I'm fine, Martha. How are you and the children?"

"The children are well and I'm getting stronger every day, thank God!" Martha sat down next to her, reached out and took Rachel's hand. "You said that you're fine, but I still think you look out of sorts. What's bothering you, Rachel?"

"What's bothering me is *me*. You remember when I told you about the soldier with the kind eyes?" Martha nodded. "Well, I haven't been able to get him out of my mind. When I shared my feelings with my mother she told me to forget about him."

"Naturally, you haven't been unable to do it. So, what have you done about it besides pine away day and night?"

"I asked Gideon to go to the garrison to find out his name. I know it was a foolish thing to do but I felt desperate."

"How in the world would Gideon know whom to ask about? He certainly couldn't have just asked about a soldier with kind eyes."

"No. Two soldiers came to our house to tell my father that they had discovered who murdered the soldier who was found near the docks. One of the soldiers told my mother that he was Captain Drusus. The other soldier happened to be the man who had helped me. I asked Gideon to go the garrison to ask Captain Drusus for the name of the soldier that came with him. Drusus told Gideon his name was Sergeant Lucius."

"So, now that you know his name, where does that get you?"

"It gets me to what I want to discuss with you. I want to know if it's all right with you if I ask Caleb to go to the garrison to deliver a letter to Sergeant Lucius for me."

Martha put her hand on Rachel's cheek. "Oh, my dear, dear, Rachel. Of course you can ask Caleb to deliver your letter for you. I'm sure he will be happy to help you any way he can. I just hope that you're not setting yourself up for a great disappointment. The soldier might not respond to your letter."

"I know, but if I don't try something he *never* will know how I feel. I'm sorry for imposing on your and Caleb's friendship, but I didn't know what else to do."

"Rachel, it would be impossible for you to impose on our friendship. I know how much you want to have a family. I see it in your eyes every time you look at my children. God grant that you'll not be heartbroken."

Chapter Eight

When Rachel arrived home her mother was out in front of the house baking bread in the stone oven. Jehoram sat in the shade, watching his mother. Her father and brothers were fishing. *This is a good chance for me to write my letter,* Rachel thought.

"How's Martha today?" Sarah asked.

"Martha said she's improving but she still needs help around the house. The baby was sound asleep most of time that I was there so I was able to do some sewing for Martha while she watched Jacob." Rachel sighed. "I'm going inside for a while to get out of the hot sun."

Rachel went into the house, grabbed a sheet of parchment, bottle of ink and a quill. She sat down at the table, and her mind went blank. She stared at the parchment for three minutes and then she began writing. "*I'm the woman you helped some time ago when you demanded your fellow soldier release me. He had threatened to take me to see your captain. I apologize for not thanking you at the time but I was frightened and ran away. I'm writing to thank you.*" She racked her brain trying to think of what else to write. "*I'm the daughter of Elhanan.*

You came to our house with Captain Drusus to tell him you caught the murderer of the dead soldier. My name is Rachel. "

She read the letter over and over, sighing in disappointment. She assumed the brief letter of thanks would never pique his interest. She felt miserable as tears began to roll down her cheeks, certain that her only hope of ever meeting him was bound to fail. *It isn't much but I don't know anything else to write.*

Sarah came in with two loaves of bread in her hands just as Rachel rolled the parchment into a thin scroll. Sarah noticed her wet cheeks. "Are you alright, Rachel? You look like you've been crying."

"It's nothing," Rachel answered, hiding the scroll under her arm. "A tiny bug flew into my eye." When her mother turned her back Rachel slipped the scroll up her loose fitting sleeve. "Would you like for me to help you with the bread?" Rachel asked.

Sarah put the bread on the table. "No, thank you, Rachel. The other bread isn't done yet."

"I promised Martha that I would stop by before mealtime to help her get it ready."

"That was nice of you, Rachel. You can take these two loaves of bread with you, and we'll have the two loaves that are still baking in the oven. They will have cooled off by then. Just make sure you're home before it gets dark. Your father was livid the last time you were late. He even threatened to send Harim after you."

"I promise," Rachel replied.

Jehoram came in and sat down next to Rachel. He leaned his crutches against the table, grabbed several dates out of a bowl on the table and put one in his mouth. Rachel laughed. "Didn't you have enough to eat this morning?"

"Yes, but that was this morning," he answered, popping the second date into his mouth.

*   *   *

Lucius was tired, hot and thirsty when he and his men dragged themselves into the garrison. Lucius walked into Drusus' quarters and poured a cup of wine. Drusus, sitting on his cot sharpening his sword with a wet stone, looked at Lucius. "Did you find the Zealots?"

"Yes, we did," Lucius answered, gulping down some wine. "Did you know that your wine's sour?"

"Forget my wine, what about the Zealots?"

"They were taken totally off guard. What was strange was the man who led us there wept when it was over. Who the devil is he?"

"He called himself a prophet." Drusus laughed. "He told me he had a dream that told him Rome would rule the entire world. He felt he had to help put an end to the Zealots. Frankly, I think he's crazy but I wasn't going to turn down his offer to betray them."

"He sounds like Brutus to me. Brutus thought he was saving the republic by murdering Julius Caesar but it only led to civil war. Traitors seldom get what they expect."

"True, but don't tell our prophet that. He might lead us to more of their camps. How many captives did you bring back?"

"None."

"*None?*"

"Those we didn't kill took their own lives. They knew if they were taken captive they would be crucified. Our losses were minimal."

Drusus glared at Lucius. "I don't believe there were no rebels who survived. I know you well enough to know when you're lying, Lucius. You let them go, didn't you? I remember how reluctant you were when we crucified them the last time. I resent your disobeying my orders. If we weren't friends I'd have you flogged. Don't let it happen again."

*   *   *

Meanwhile Elhanan and his two sons pulled their filled net into the boat. Elhanan bent over backwards to stretch his stiff muscles as he looked at Harim. "By the way, Harim, how is Nahash doing on his house? You never did tell us." For a few seconds Harim didn't know why his father asked such a question. Then he suddenly remembered that he had used it as an excuse when he went to join his friends. He had no idea at all how much progress Nahash had made on his house.

"Not bad," Harim answered, tossing the net into the water. "The walls are all up but they haven't started the roof yet."

Gideon looked at Harim without saying anything. He had gone passed Nahash's house since Harim supposedly had gone there and they *hadn't* finished all the walls. He realized Harim had lied about going there. Gideon glanced at his father anxiously to see if his face registered any surprise in case he also had seen Nahash's house. He breathed a sigh of relieve when his father seemed satisfied with Harim's answer.

They pulled the net back into the boat and dumped more fish into the growing pile of fish. Harim was about to toss the empty net back into the water but Elhanan stepped on it. Harim glanced at him with a startled expression.

"I guess they must not have liked the way the walls were situated," Elhanan said. "Otherwise, I don't know why they would have knocked down the walls to do it all over again."

Harim's shoulders sagged in guilt, realizing his father knew that he had lied. He didn't know what to say. He waited for his father to confront him for lying, but it wasn't necessary. Elhanan merely looked at him in disappointment. "Well, Harim, throw the net into the water."

Meanwhile, Rachel went to the docks to wait for Caleb. She felt awkward pacing back and forth. She looked down the beach and saw a stranger and a dozen other men getting out of a boat. A number of people rushed over and greeted them in excitement. Fascinated as to what was going on, she joined them. She wondered what the stranger meant when he said, *"I will make you fishers of men."*

Rachel wanted to hear more but spotted a small fishing boat in the distance coming toward shore. He was too far out for her to recognize who it was. She whispered a prayer of thanksgiving when she was certain it was Caleb. Neither one spoke when he reached the dock, but she noticed him smiling at her. After he tethered his boat to the dock he unloaded his fish into a cart. Rachel fondled her letter in one hand, holding a sheepskin pouch with two loaves of bread in the other hand. She watched Caleb untie the boat, pull it down the shoreline twenty or more feet and then drag it onto the beach.

Rachel stood by his cart when he walked back to get it. "From that look on your face, Rachel, I take it that Martha gave her approval."

"Yes, just as you said she would. I'll give you the letter when we reach your home. Are you sure you don't mind taking my letter to the garrison?"

"Not only don't I mind, I'm happy to be of help to you. Besides, Martha wouldn't forgive me if I changed my mind after she agreed it was something she wanted me to do."

Caleb saw one of his friends. "Wait a minute, Sallai!" he called out, pushing his cart over to him. "I have something important to do and can't take my fish to Mesech to be sold. Would you be willing to drop my fish off at Mesech's for me?"

"I'd be glad to. I was already going that way."

"Thanks, Sallai."

Caleb and Rachel walked towards Caleb's house as she handed him the letter. They went into the house and saw Martha sitting at the table holding the baby. He kissed the baby and his wife, and then gulped down two glasses of water.

Rachel opened the pouch and put the loaves of bread on the table.

"Mother sent these with me," Rachel said. "I told her that I was making your meal for tonight. Now, what would you like? I don't want to brag but I'm a fantastic cook."

Martha laughed. "Whatever you do best, Rachel, as long as it's something we have in the house. The means it will have to be salted fish, figs, honey and cabbage. Plus, of course, your mother's bread."

"I want to wash the salt water and sweat off before I go to the garrison," Caleb said. When Joshua ran up to him he picked him up, kissed his cheek and put him down. He looked at Martha. "I doubt that I'll be gone long."

Caleb walked out the door, dumped some water over his head from a bucket and headed for the garrison. Two guards stopped Caleb when he arrived at the garrison's gate. They were the same two who had detained Elhanan and Harim.

"I'd like to talk with Sergeant Lucius," Caleb said.

One of the guards turned to scan the courtyard. He spotted Lucius and two other soldiers sitting on a stone bench in the shade of a palm tree. The guard pointed in their direction. "He's the one on the left side of the bench."

The guards watched Caleb walk over to the three soldiers. "Excuse me, Sergeant Lucius, but I have a letter for you. My name is Caleb and I'm a friend of Elhanan. His daughter Rachel asked me to give this to you."

Lucius, remembering Elhanan's name, took the scroll and opened it. "Elhanan's daughter, you say." He read the letter and scratched the top of his head. "She wrote in the letter that I helped her, but I don't remember it. What does she look like?"

"Like a Jewish woman," Caleb answered, smiling. "She's young, about five foot five, has wavy, black hair down to her shoulders." Caleb, not having read the letter, repeated part of what it said. "Rachel told me that one of your fellow soldiers threatened to take her to your captain. She said that you stopped him and told him to let her go."

"Oh yes, now I remember her. I didn't know she was Elhanan's daughter. Why didn't she say something when I went there with my captain to tell Elhanan that we caught our killer?"

"Rachel told me that she wasn't home when you went there."

"I see," Lucius replied, rolling up the letter. "Tell Rachel that it was my pleasure. Thanks for bringing me her letter, Caleb."

Rachel waited anxiously for Caleb to return as she prepared the evening meal for his family. As soon as Caleb walked in the door Martha asked, "Well, Caleb, tell us what happened?"

Caleb looked at Rachel. "I gave Sergeant Lucius your letter, Rachel. He read it and asked me about you. When I explained to him who you were he seemed quite pleased and told me that it was his pleasure to have helped you."

Martha took the bowl of cabbage from her. "I can handle this, Rachel. You better go home before it gets dark."

Rachel started for the door but stopped to look back at Caleb. "Thank you, Caleb, for what you did for me."

*   *   *

When Elhanan, Harim and Gideon arrived home after taking care of their catch of fish, the family sat down for their evening meal. Apart from greeting the other members of the family, Elhanan and Harim barely spoke. Even young Jehoram sensed the tension between them. Sarah and Rachel guessed that they must have had another argument. After their meal Harim went outside and sat down on a bench. Jehoram hobbled out on his crutches and sat down next to him.

"You and father had an argument, didn't you?" Jehoram asked. Harim grinned, but didn't say anything. "I wish you and father didn't disagree so much," Jehoram said. "It makes me sad to see that you two can't get along."

Harim rubbed the top of Jehoram's head. "I know that, Jehoram. Don't let it bother you so much. Father and I still love each other. It's just that he seems so willing to accommodate Rome's oppression. That's the sort of weakness that enables them to hold our people under their thumb."

"I don't care about politics. I care about our family and I'm afraid you're tearing our family apart." Jehoram looked Harim. "Besides, you're not being fair. Father's a fisherman, not a soldier. What do you expect him to do?"

"I don't expect him to *do* anything. I only wish he wouldn't try to stop me from associating with my friends." Harim saw tears building in Jehoram's eyes and felt sorry for him. "You're only seven years old Jehoram and can't understand the way I feel."

Jehoram wiped his eyes with his knuckles. "I *don't* understand! All that I know is you and father are not as close as you used to be, and I wish you were."

Rachel came out just as Harim stood up. "I think I'll go for a walk down to the water and watch the sunset," Harim said. "Want to come along Jehoram?"

Jehoram pushed himself up with his crutches to join Harim. Rachel sat down on the empty bench and watched them walk away. Her mind was on Caleb's brief message. *What should I do now that Lucius read my letter? Caleb told me that Lucius seemed pleased with my letter and was glad to have helped me. That's hardly an indication that he might like to meet me.*

She wasn't there with her private thoughts for long before Gideon came out. "Where did Harim and Jehoram go?" he asked in disappointment. "I thought they were out here."

"They went down to the sea to watch the sunset," Rachel answered.

"I wish I knew that they were going down there," Gideon said, sitting down next to Rachel. "I would have gone with them." He noticed she looked distracted. "If you're thinking about why father and Harim were so quiet at supper, I can tell you. Father caught Harim in a lie."

"What lie?"

"When we came back from fishing two days ago Harim said he wanted to go see how Nahash's house was coming along. But when father asked him about it today Harim said the walls were finished. Father had seen Nahash's house and knew Harim had lied."

"Oh, no. How could Harim be so stupid?" Rachel sighed, and looked at Gideon. "Actually, Gideon, that wasn't what I was thinking about. I asked Caleb to take a letter to Sergeant Lucius for me. Lucius told Caleb that he was pleased with my letter and was glad to have helped me."

Gideon felt disappointed Rachel had asked Caleb rather than him to deliver her letter, but didn't say so. "What did you write in your letter?"

"Only that I wanted to thank him for helping me and that I am Elhanan's daughter. I didn't know what else to write. I *wanted* to suggest that we might meet sometime but wasn't sure how he would react." She closed her eyes and tilted her head back. "Now I think that I made a foolish mistaken in writing the letter."

"I don't think it was a mistake, Rachel. He at least now knows your name and that you appreciated his help. After all, Caleb did say that Lucius was pleased."

Sarah came out of the house. "Where's Jehoram?" she asked. "I thought he was out here."

I hope mother didn't hear us mention Lucius' name, Rachel thought. She looked up at her mother. "He went with Harim to watch the sunset down by the water."

Sarah shrugged her shoulders, turned around and went back into the house. "Is there anything that I can do to help,

Rachel?" Gideon whispered. "I could go back to the garrison to tell Lucius that you would like to talk with him."

"No, Gideon, you've done enough for me already. Thank you for offering but now I'll leave it up to God's providence. If it's God's will Lucius will have to do the rest."

* * *

News about the massacre of the Zealots near Chorazin spread rapidly throughout Capernaum. The entire Jewish population was devastated. Many were terrified the Romans would punish anyone else they suspected of having any ties with the Zealots even if they were innocent. A minority wanted revenge but didn't intend to do anything. A smaller minority *did* plan to do something.

Chapter Nine

When Elhanan and his two sons returned from fishing several days later Gideon's friend, Ishbak, was nearby throwing stones into the sea. Gideon didn't say anything as he glanced at his father. Gideon's eyes spoke for him. Elhanan smiled and said, "Go on, Gideon. Harim and I'll take care of the fish."

Gideon thanked his father and dashed off to join Ishbak in his carefree activity. "Don't you have to help your father and brother?" Ishbak asked.

"My father said I didn't need to." Gideon picked up a pebble and tossed it into the water as far as he could. "Let's see you beat that throw!"

The two friends worked their way several hundred yards down the shore trying to outdo each other throwing stones as far as possible. Each one claimed to have won with each attempt, but it didn't matter. They enjoyed the contest just for the fun of it. Ishbak noticed a dozen or so men getting out of a boat about fifty yards further down the shore. Gideon wasn't aware that Rachel had seen a similar event two weeks earlier. Nor did he know that Rachel had heard Jesus a number of times since.

"That looks like the rabbi we saw some time ago walking through the street with a crowd following him," Ishbak said. "The man they called Jesus." Gideon glanced down the beach and picked up a stone as if he wasn't interested. "What's the matter, Gideon? I thought you were interested in Jesus."

Gideon threw the stone into the water. "My father and brother said he is a false prophet who deceives people and breaks our laws."

"That's what Elizabad's father had said but you still seemed interested in hearing about Jesus. What changed your mind?"

"I just told you. I didn't believe Elizabad's father at the time but that was before I talked with my father and brother. I believe them."

"Well, my older brother, Jubal, heard Jesus teaching a number of times and insists Jesus is a great prophet. Jubal told me that Jesus teaches about God's Kingdom, not Satan. You know that Jubal isn't easily impressed with religious teachers, Gideon, but Jesus really impressed my brother."

"My father and brother know more than Jubal. If Jubal listened to our teachers more he wouldn't be so gullible about false teachers. He would do better to listen to Rabbi Jacobs who teaches according to our laws."

After three minutes of silent stone throwing Ishbak changed subjects. "Did your parents ever find out about our going to the Roman garrison for your sister?"

"No, and I hope they never do. They have no idea she's interested in a soldier, but I know they would be terribly angry if they ever found out."

*   *   *

A growing number of Jewish leaders were concerned that more and more of their people were following Jesus.

So was Captain Drusus. Their reasons differed. Some Pharisees thought Jesus was breaking their traditions, and a number of Saducees were jealous of their position. For Drusus, large crowds of Jews represented potential problems that he hoped to avoid. He had heard a number of different stories about Jesus and was determined to find out the truth from a more reliable source.

He summoned Lucius to his quarters following his morning meal. "I'm tired of hearing all sorts of tales about this Jesus who has been attracting larger crowds," Drusus said. "I don't want a problem with the Jews like Herod had after he killed John the Baptist. I want you to take one man with you and go listen to what Jesus is saying first hand. I want to know if he says anything treasonous."

"Do you want to me to arrest him if he does?"

"Not when he's with a crowd, I don't. That might cause a riot. I understand Jesus usually hangs around with twelve men after the crowds disperse. Find out where they stay when they are in Capernaum. If Jesus talks treason I want you to bring him to me for questioning."

Lucius walked out of Drusus' quarters without saying anything. *The first thing I need to do is to find out where Jesus is,* Lucius thought. He walked up to six of his men sitting in the shade drinking wine. "There's a Jew by the name of Jesus who wanders throughout Galilee speaking to large crowds," Lucius said. "Find out where he will be speaking. Don't do anything but come back to tell me where I can go hear him."

Four hours later one of the soldiers entered Lucius' quarters. "Jesus was last seen about half a mile southwest of the city. According to a Jewish woman Jesus was headed this way. She said Jesus usually speaks on the hillside north of the synagogue."

"Jesus might be there by now. Then again, he might not even go there. I want you to go and wait for him. If Jesus arrives come tell me at once."

When the soldier got there he saw a large crowd climbing the hillside. He asked a man, "What's going on?"

The man looked at the soldier, wondering why he wanted to know. "Jesus of Nazareth is coming to speak to the people," the man answered.

The soldier turned, ran to the garrison and walked up to Lucius' open door. "Well, what did you find out?" Lucius asked.

"A man told me Jesus is on his way to talk to the people."

Lucius stood up and put on his helmet. "Good. Come with me."

Twenty minutes later Lucius and the soldier saw that a large crowd had already gathered on the hillside. Lucius stopped and gazed at the crowd in amazement. "By Jove, there must be over a thousand people here! No wonder Drusus is concerned. I wonder what this Jesus could say that would attract so many?"

Lucius and the soldier climbed the hill, stopped when they couldn't get closer and looked around at the peaceful scene. "This crowd doesn't look anything like a mob of potential troublemakers," Lucius said. "Not only are there as many women as men, there are young children, too."

Then he noticed three Sadducees and two Pharisees standing next to each other in their elegant robes. "That's remarkable considering they don't like each other," Lucius said, pointing them out to the soldier. "I distrust those legalistic characters. I wonder what they think of Jesus?" He laughed. "From their grim expressions, I take it that it isn't favorable."

Lucius listened to Jesus speak as he continued to scan the crowd. Although they failed to notice each other, Rachel was also there listening to Jesus. Everyone began to sit down on the ground to listen. Lucius sighed. "I guess Jesus must usually speak for quite a while."

Lucius, wanting to hear what Jesus had to say, made sure he sat close enough to hear most of it. Jesus spoke without being interrupted and then answered questions by the people. *There isn't anything that can be considered treasonous in what Jesus is saying,* Lucius thought. *He only talks about forgiveness, hope, God's Kingdom and repentance.* Lucius didn't know who the Father of Jesus was, but overheard a man say in a demeaning tone that Jesus was the son of a carpenter. *Does that matter?* Lucius thought.

When it was over the crowd calmly got up to make their way home. No one appeared riled-up or agitated by what they heard. There had been no words calling for insurrection. Lucius went to the garrison to report to Drusus what he had learned.

Drusus, rubbing down his magnificent black horse in the stable, saw Lucius headed for his quarters. "Over here Lucius!"

Lucius walked over and stroked the horse's nose. "Well, I heard Jesus. We have nothing to worry about. He's nothing more than an idealistic teacher who talked about His God. He said nothing that sounded the least like rebellion."

Drusus slapped his horse's rump. "I'm glad to hear it, but I want you to keep an eye on him for a while. No matter how innocent it sounded this time there's always the chance that he might change his tune once he has more followers." They walked toward Drusus' quarters. "By the way, how many were there?" Drusus asked.

"I'd estimate over a thousand, but many were women and children."

Drusus looked at him with a stunned expression. "That many! I hope you're right about his not being a troublemaker."

"I did see something interesting. Three Sadducees and two Pharisees huddled together. By the look on their faces they were not pleased with Jesus' teaching."

"I've never known them to agree on anything. Maybe they were jealous of the large crowds following Jesus. I wouldn't put it past *them* to cause trouble even if Jesus doesn't. The next time you hear Jesus make sure you keep an eye of them, too. I don't trust that lot."

"Neither do I."

*   *   *

Over the next three days Lucius heard Jesus on two more occasions. He was more and more convinced that Jesus had no intention of inspiring a revolt against Rome. In fact, he found himself attracted by Jesus' words. After the third time of listening to Jesus he thought he recognized someone as the crowd began to disperse. He studied her face, trying to remember who she was.

Unable to place her, he walked over to her and smiled. "I think I've seen you before, but I don't know where?"

Rachel, recognizing him at once, blushed. "I'm Elhanan's daughter, Rachel."

"That's right, now I remember. You sent me a letter recently for helping you. According to your letter I stopped one of my men from harassing you when we questioned you about someone." They started walking together. "That was before I met your father. How is he by the way?"

Her heart pounded with excitement. "My father's fine, thank you. He was surprised how fairly your captain treated him."

Lucius laughed. "Well, he couldn't have been more surprised than my captain was with your father's courage. I doubt many men would have gone to the garrison to report the murder of a soldier the way your father did. Drusus, that's my captain, was impressed by your father and that isn't easy to do."

They strolled along without speaking until he asked, "What are you doing here Rachel? Are you a follower of this Jesus?"

"Not really, but I've heard Him speak several times." Rachel suddenly felt alarmed. "Why are you here?"

"Captain Drusus ordered me to listen to what Jesus was saying. He tends to be uneasy when large crowds follow someone he doesn't know anything about." Lucius glanced at Rachel and laughed. "And Jesus is attracting *very* large crowds. Would you mind if I walked you home?"

I'd like nothing more than for you to walk me home but it's impossible, Rachel thought. *My family would be livid to see us together.* She sighed. "I wish that you could but I'm afraid you better not."

"I know. Jews and Romans don't walk together without making enemies of their family and friends. Tell me, Rachel, what do you think about Jesus?"

"I know there are many of our people who believe Jesus is a false prophet, but I like what He teaches. He talks about forgiveness, faith in God and hope. I don't see how people could possibly think that such things are false. What do you think about Him?"

"You might find this hard to believe from a Roman soldier, Rachel, but I've agreed with everything I heard Jesus say each time I heard Him."

When Rachel felt him take her hand in his she squeezed his hand in response. "How many times have you heard Jesus?" she asked.

"This was the third time."

"You must really like Him to hear Him that often."

"I didn't choose to go listen to Him, Rachel. I was ordered to by my captain."

"I forgot that you already told me that. I'm sorry I asked you. I should have remembered that you don't necessarily do what you want to do."

Lucius smiled at her. "You don't have to apologize to me, Rachel. Regardless of my original purpose for listening to Jesus, I told you the truth when I said that I believed what He taught. I don't consider Jesus an enemy any more than you do. Believe it or not, Rome doesn't think most Jews are enemies."

"Strange you should say that, Lucius, because I never thought of you as an enemy from the very first day I saw you. But my family will *never* understand that as long we are a conquered people."

"We don't conquer nations so we can destroy them or their way of life, Rachel. We want them to become a part of a great empire. People can still worship their own gods and live the way they want as long as they're also loyal to Rome."

"I hope you can understand how *we* feel," Rachel replied, sighing. "Our culture, like our religion, isn't easily forsaken just so we can be engulfed into another nation's vision of the future. We believe God called us centuries ago to be unique. Unity might sound good to Rome, but we believe we'd lose our identity if we abandoned our heritage."

"All I'm saying, Rachel, is that it isn't our intention to destroy your way of life. Other nations who have adapted themselves to the inevitable have prospered more than they ever did. Our roads, common language and trade have made them stronger, not weaker. I'm afraid that this Jewish stubbornness is only making things harder on your people."

"I wish you could understand how our people feel. Even if Rome's *intentions* are for our benefit the price is too high. What you called stubbornness, we call faithfulness. What Rome sees as strength, we see as weakness in religious commitment. Rome's desire for stability only comes through oppression. It offers peace, but at a very high price."

"I just hope your peoples' faithfulness doesn't eventually lead to more unnecessary deaths. I really do! I agree that peace comes at a high price, but tragically so does rebellion."

They reached the place where Rachel had to turn toward home. They stopped walking as he took both her hands in his, looking into her eyes. "May I see you again?"

"It would break my heart if you didn't want to see me again."

"I'm glad to hear you say so. I'll make a point of coming to hear Jesus the next time he speaks. If you're able to do the same we can talk again then."

"I promise you that I will."

Lucius released her hand and watched her walk away. He sighed and went to tell Drusus what he heard this time from Jesus. When he went into Drusus' quarters to report, Drusus shared some disturbing news with Lucius before he could open his mouth about Jesus.

"A Jew came here to tell me that a man called Zedekiah is trying to unite the various bands of Zealots in Galilee into an army. The Jew insisted that he didn't know where Zedekiah was or where they were meeting. When I asked him why he came to tell me about it, he said that he was trying to prevent a bloodbath before Zedekiah managed to lead more people into his plan."

Lucius' entire body sagged in despair. It was the *last* thing he wanted to hear after his talk with Rachel. "Was it the same man who led us to Chorazin?" he asked.

"No, but his motive was the same. His name is Zephaniah. He has met with the Zealots several times. Obviously there are plenty of Jews who feel the Zealots are as harmful to living in peace as much as we do."

I think the man we were looking for when I first saw Rachel was called Zedekiah, Lucius thought. "Did you believe Zephaniah?"

"Of course. He would hardly want to make up such a story if it wasn't true. I want you to find this Zedekiah before he succeeds."

"You said that Zephaniah didn't where we could find Zedekiah."

"True, but he said he'd tell us the next time they planned on meeting."

*   *   *

Over the next several weeks Lucius and Rachel met five more times on the hillside where they first saw each other after listening to Jesus speak. Lucius had ordered two of his men to find out what they could about Zedekiah, but discovered nothing about his whereabouts. Lucius, hoping Zephaniah had lied in what he had told Drusus, hadn't said a word to Rachel about it.

Martha had improved enough that she didn't need her nearly as much. Rachel, happy for Martha's family, allowed her mother to assume that she was spending all the time at Martha's when in fact she was meeting with Lucius. One hot afternoon Lucius and Rachel sat in the shade of a cypress tree with her head on his shoulder, admiring the tranquil view of fishing boats sailing on the sea in the distance. Rachel knew her father and brothers were on one of them.

Lucius sighed and asked a question he knew had to be asked sooner or later. "When do you think you'll tell your family about us, Rachel? They eventually will have to know that we love each other."

"Oh, Lucius, you have no idea how much I *want* to tell them about you," she said sadly, looking into his blue eyes. "But I'm afraid once I tell them about you they'll realize I have been meeting with you instead of being with Martha. They might forbid me from leaving the house on my own."

"Do they hate Romans that much?"

"It's *not* just that you are a Roman, Lucius. You could be a Greek or Egyptian and it wouldn't matter. My parents are determined that I should only marry a Jew. Please don't think badly about them. It's just that Jews don't believe of marrying outside our faith."

"I've never been able to understand that. You Jews are the only people in the world who insist on not marrying other races. So what are we to do? I can't change who or what I am, now can I?"

"I'll tell them but I need more time to decide *how* to tell them," she answered, sighing. "I'm not sure how my father will react but I know that my mother will object strongly. And I have a brother who hates all Romans."

Lucius sensed her Rachel's alarm when her body grew tense. "Relax, Rachel. You don't have to be afraid of me on your brother's account. There are many Jews who hate us with a passion, but we don't arrest people for the way they feel. Your brother is quite safe as long as he keeps his hatred to himself and doesn't do something foolish."

She turned her head and kissed him on the cheek. "I'll try to muster up enough courage to tell my parents soon. You know how much I love you. Just be patient with me a little longer."

"I'll be more patient with you than Drusus will be with me if I don't follow his orders," Lucius replied, getting up. "He wants me to talk with your Rabbi Jacobs about Jesus." He helped Rachel to her feet. "It seems Rabbi Jacobs complained to Drusus that Jesus is trying to stir up trouble against Rome. I already told Drusus that Jesus is interested in religion, not politics. But Drusus *is* interested in politics and wants to keep peace with Rabbi Jacobs."

After they embraced they walked slowly down the hill toward Rachel's home. When they reluctantly parted Lucius went to see Rabbi Jacobs as she continued going home. Rabbi Jacobs was returning home after teaching his class the *Torah* at the synagogue. He was a tall, slim man in his late fifties with a heavy beard and curly black hair.

Lucius, seeing Rabbi Jacobs, called out to him. "Wait a minute, Rabbi, I want to talk with you." Lucius walked up to the rabbi. "I'm Sergeant Lucius. Captain Drusus told me that you said a man called Jesus has been trying to create problems with Rome. When did this supposedly happen?"

"It didn't *supposedly* happen, Sergeant Lucius, it did happen! In fact, it happens every time Jesus speaks. He not only tells people they don't have to pay taxes to Rome, Jesus insists that He's a king. I'm sure that you know Caesar appointed Herod king, not Jesus."

"Well, I've heard Jesus eight times and He *never* said any such thing," Lucius replied, glaring at Rabbi Jacobs. "As far as taxes are concerned Jesus said the exact opposite of what you asserted. When a man asked Him about taxes I personally heard Jesus say that we are to render to Caesar that which is his. Understand this, Rabbi, when you try to cause trouble between Jesus' followers and the rest of the Jews in Galilee, it is *you* who is breeding contention among your people, not Jesus."

"Then you obviously haven't heard Jesus enough. I told you what He said. If you don't want your captain to know what's going on around him that's your mistake, not mine for trying to warn him."

"Oh, you can count on my telling Captain Drusus *who* is the troublemaker," Lucius said, continuing to glare at him. With that he turned and walked away, leaving Rabbi Jacobs to interpret what was meant by his parting remark.

When Lucius walked into the garrison he was surprised to see a man tied to a post. The man's unconscious head was dropped forward on his chest, his bareback baring bloody marks from a brutal lashing. Lucius went to see Drusus to find out what had happened.

Drusus sat at his desk eating a melon. He watched Lucius walk in and sit down. "Where the devil have you been, Lucius?" he asked in a testy tone

"I went to talk with Rabbi Jacobs as you ordered. The rabbi told me Jesus teaches people to refuse to pay taxes, but I know for a fact that he lied about that. I heard Jesus say people are supposed to pay their taxes. He also accused Jesus of saying other things that I know were lies."

"I thought as much. The rabbi struck me as a power hungry man who would resent anyone attracting Jews more than he could."

"I saw a man in the courtyard strapped to a pole," Lucius said. "What's that all about?"

"He isn't just any man, Lucius, he's a Zealot. Two of our men stopped him from taking a cartload of swords buried under a pile of wood outside the city. We persuaded him to tell us where he was taking them." Lucius knew how they had *persuaded* him. "He also confessed that Zedekiah is meeting with about a hundred of his traitors tonight at dusk in the woods outside the city."

"Then Zephaniah told us the truth about Zedekiah."

"He did. We have him, Lucius. We finally have Zedekiah. I want you to take 500 of your men to arrest them, but give them half an hour before you do. I want to make sure they all have time to get there. Try to bring back Zedekiah alive if possible. If he has been trying to organize various groups of Zealots we might be able to persuade to tell us where the other groups are located."

There were some things that Lucius liked about the army, some that he felt ambivalent about and some that he despised. He liked the sense of purpose it gave to his life and the friendships with his fellow soldiers. He tolerated the tedium that dominated so much of the time, but he *despised* what he had just been ordered to do. Fighting a disciplined army prepared for battle was one thing, but ambushing an unexpecting handful of foolish non-soldiers was another.

Lucius rose to his feet and walked toward the door as Drusus said, "Remember what I told you about letting them go free."

Lucius glanced back at him and then walked out. It was a warm, breezeless evening with a full moon later that night. When Lucius and his men reached the edge of the woods Lucius raised his hand to signal a halt. Lucius turned to Gnaeus. "I want twenty of our men to spread out and go into the woods thirty or forty yards apart as quietly as possible. Tell them to stop when they hear voices. Then come back here to tell us where the rebels are meeting."

Twenty minutes later a soldier came back. "I heard them, Captain," he said pointing to his left. "They're between six and seven hundred yards that direction."

"All right," Lucius whispered to Gnaeus, "this is what we'll do. We'll swing around in both directions until we form a circle around the area. I'll go to the right and you take half the men and go left. Warn your men to be careful they don't make any noise. When your men are in place yell that you're ready, and move forward."

The soldiers crept through the woods as quietly as possible. When Gnaeus gave the signal Lucius shouted, "Stay where you are or die!"

When the soldiers charged forward the astonished Jews glanced around for a way to escape but there wasn't any. Some who panicked ran straight into the swords of the soldiers. Fifty-three confused patriots tried to fight their way out of the trap only to fall dead before the more skilled soldiers. The brief struggle was fierce. A dozen or so Jews escaped into the dark woods. Twenty-nine were taken back to the garrison as prisoners.

By the time they marched their prisoners into the garrison it was dark and late. Lucius paid no attention to their faces when they were led in mass into the crowded prison. Lucius went to his quarters and drank until he passed out.

Meanwhile, Elhanan and his family worried why Harim hadn't returned home that night. Making things worse, none of them had any idea where he had gone.

Chapter Ten

When Harim still hadn't come home the next morning Sarah was worried. Elhanan was not surprised when Sarah suggested, "Rather than going fishing without Harim, I think you should try to find him." She had tears in her eyes.

Harim has most likely been with his friends and fallen asleep in a drunken stupor somewhere, Elhanan thought. He wanted to lash out at Harim for causing Sarah so much anxiety, but Sarah's tears kept him from telling her what he thought.

"Gideon and I will try to find out where he is," Elhanan replied, "but if he comes home while we're gone tell him not to go anywhere until I talk with him. He has some explaining to do."

Elhanan and Gideon spent the entire morning looking for Harim. They couldn't find him anywhere. *Even if Harim was drunk last night he should be around here somewhere,* Elhanan thought, trying to suppress his anxiety. *Harim didn't merely fall asleep. He's in some kind of trouble.*

Rachel had stayed with her mother. "Listen, Rachel, your watching over me like a hen over her eggs is only making me more nervous," Sarah said. "You can't do anything here, and Martha might need you. Why don't you go give her a hand?"

"I think I should stay here with you."

"I appreciate what you trying to do, but it won't help. I'll let you know if Harim comes home or I hear anything from your father."

Rachel took off her apron, walked over and kissed her mother on the check. "I'm sure Harim is okay," she said with more confidence than she felt. "God is with Harim wherever he is. I won't be gone long."

Rachel was halfway to Martha's when she saw two of her friends standing on the dusty road in front of her talking. They sounded frantic. Rachel rushed over to them and asked, "What on earth is the matter?"

Deborah answered between deep sobs, "The Roman soldiers . . . slaughtered over a hundred of our men . . . last night. It was horrible! I heard . . . they also arrested dozens of survivors . . . and plan on crucifying them."

Rachel's knees buckled in shock. "Oh my God, no!" she screamed. "My brother, Harim, didn't come home last." She grabbed Deborah's arm. "Are you sure?"

"Yes. My uncle, Michael, came to our house early this morning. He told us he overheard a man who had managed to escape talking about it." Before Deborah had the chance to say more Rachel turned and ran toward the garrison.

When she got there it was obvious that word had spread rapidly. A large group of people stood at the gate begging for information about those being held. Four guards held them back with their swords. The crowd yelling at the same time sounded incoherent. Rachel recognized one of the soldiers whom she had seen several times with Lucius. She tried to push her way passed the crowd, but couldn't reach him. She waved her hand back and forth until he noticed her.

When he did she shouted as loud as she could, "Tell Sergeant Lucius that I need to talk with him!"

Recognizing her as a friend of Lucius, he turned and walked away. A few moments later Lucius arrived and worked his way back to Rachel. He took her by the arm and led her away from the crowd. "Rachel, what the devil are you doing here?"

"Oh, Lucius, is it true that a hundred Jews were killed last night and that you intend to crucify those who were taken prisoners?"

"Yes, it's true but why are you so shaken? You're white as a sheet."

She stopped walking, covered her face with her hands and sobbed. When she finally could speak, she said, looking at him through her tears, "My brother, Harim, didn't come home last night. I'm afraid he might have been killed or arrested."

Lucius' eyes opened wide, fearing the worst. *What will she think of me if she knew I was the man who was in charge of the attack?* He put his hand on her shoulder. "He might not have been there, Rachel," he said.

"Can you find out for me?"

"I'll find out the names of those who were killed but that will take some time. I'll check out who was arrested right away. A few did manage to escape. If your brother *was* there maybe he was among those who got away." He held his breath, thinking, *I'm a fool for saying that. How would I know some escaped if I wasn't there?* He hoped Rachel hadn't realized the same thing.

Rachel blotted her wet eyes with her sleeve. Then she pushed his hand away, stepping back. "I better go tell my family about what happened last night," she said, sounding bitter.

The sight of Lucius in his uniform made her feel like a traitor to her family and neighbors. Rachel glared at him as if he were a stranger to be feared, but she didn't ask him how he knew about the escapees. Lucius didn't know what to say. She slowly backed away more and more before she turned and ran home.

Lucius wanted to call after her. "All I could do now is find out about what happened to Harim," he muttered under his breath.

As she rushed home she decided to tell only part of what had happened, leaving out any reference about talking with Lucius. When she arrived home Elhanan and Gideon were already there. Harim's absence and their expression told her they had failed to find Harim. Rachel walked into the house and collapsed on a chair. Her face was white and she shook from head to foot.

Sarah sat down next to her, took her hand and stared at her. "What's the matter, Rachel? You look like you've seen an evil spirit?"

Rachel, feeling nauseated, took several deep breaths as Sarah squeezed her hand. Rachel looked at her mother through blurred red eyes. "I met Deborah and Judith on the way to Martha's." She took several more breaths. "Deborah said her uncle told her that the soldiers attacked a number of Jews last night."

Sarah gasped and covered her mouth with both hands as Elhanan moved behind Jehoram, putting his hands on his shoulders. "According to Deborah's uncle, the soldiers killed over a hundred men and plan on crucifying those taken prisoners."

Elhanan plopped onto a chair next to Jehoram in shock. Sarah lowered her head onto her arms resting on the table, sobbing deeply. Gideon went over, leaned over his mother's back and hugged her.

Jehoram, having failed to make the connection between what Rachel had said with Harim's absence, was confused by everyone's reaction. "What's wrong?" he asked innocently. "Why is everyone so upset?"

Elhanan reached out, pulled Jehoram onto his lap and held him tight. "We're not positive, Jehoram, but there's a chance Harim has gotten himself in serious trouble," he answered. He looked at Sarah. "I'll go to the garrison to ask Captain Drusus if he knows anything about Harim."

"No, Father, you don't have to do that," Rachel said without thinking.

Elhanan looked at her in surprise. "What do you mean by that?"

"I already did. I was out of my mind with fear and already went to the garrison. I had no idea what I was going to do, but Captain Drusus was talking with the crowd at the gate when I got there. He told them he would post the names of the prisoners on the garrison's gate as soon as he had a list of their names."

* * *

Lucius immediately headed for the soldier guarding the prison. He knew that if Harim had been among those present in the woods the odds were that he wouldn't have been arrested or escaped, but most likely killed.

"I want a list of the names of those you have in prison," Lucius told the guard. "I'll be back shortly to pick it up."

Lucius turned away and went straight to Captain Drusus' quarters. Drusus was in the mist of a heated argument with three influential representatives of the Jewish community. "We beg for clemency for the prisoners," one of the Jews said. "Flog them if you must, but don't crucify them."

Drusus stood behind his desk leaning forward on his knuckles. "The Zealots knew what the punishment was for treason," he growled. "Rome does *not* threaten to do something and then back away from it when revolutionaries get caught. You had your say, now get out!"

The three petitioners walked passed Lucius on the way out of Drusus' quarters. Drusus sat down in disgust and looked at Lucius. "When will these cursed Jews learn that we mean what we say?" He pushed the wine jug toward Lucius. "Sit down and pour yourself some wine."

Lucius knew that if Harim *was* a prisoner the only way he could help him was to convince Drusus that it was to his advantage to release him. Lucius poured some wine, sat down and took a deep breath. "I don't know, Drusus, maybe it would be better if we were merciful this time. When we crucified the Zealots the last time it didn't stop other men from plotting revolt. The Jews might be impressed with such leniency."

Drusus laughed. "You can't be serious! If we showed any weakness it would only lead more fools to think they might get away with treason. You surprise me, Lucius. I know you didn't like it when we crucified them before. I also remember the last time you let the wounded men go, but you never suggested that I should be lenient before. What's gotten into you recently?"

"Nothing. I just don't think it's necessary, that's all. We already demonstrated our strength and resolve last night when we killed a hundred Zealots. Killing twenty-nine unarmed men will hardly make us look *more* formidable. Perhaps the Jews would be more willing to accept Rome's rule if we were less ruthless."

"No, Lucius. Mercy is the same as weakness, and weakness invariably leads to rebellion."

"True, but strength doesn't require cruelty. Rome has prided itself on justice for centuries by banishing those who committed crimes."

"You know better than that, Lucius. Rome only banishes Roman citizens, not traitors from other nations. Augustus banished his own daughter and adopted son, Postumus, but he never banished a non-Roman."

Lucius, realizing he wasn't about to change Drusus' mind, stood up and walked out of Drusus' quarters without saying anything more. He took several steps, stopped and covered his face with his hand knowing he was letting Rachel down. Then he went to find out the names of the prisoners. The guard handed him the list of names.

Lucius read down the list until he saw *Harim, son of Elhanan* half way down the list. He sighed, tilted his head back and closed his eyes, remembering Rachel's expression when she had backed away from him. Lucius knew he had no choice but to tell Rachel about Harim.

Lucius walked to within a stone's throw of her house and stopped. *I can't just walk up to Rachel's house and ask to talk with Rachel,* he thought. A young Jewish boy, about ten or eleven-years-old, was carrying a basket of apples headed in the opposite direction.

Lucius stopped him. "I would like for you to do a favor for me," he said. He pulled a coin out of his pouch and handed it to the boy. "Here's a silver coin." He pointed at Rachel's house. "I want you go to that house and tell a woman by the name of Rachel that Lucius wants to talk with her."

The youngster clasped the coin tightly in his hand, smiled and did as he was told. When Rachel came out she looked around for Lucius. She spotted him waving at her next to a tree and ran toward him, praying silently that Lucius had good news. When she was close enough to see the gloomy expression on his face she knew that it wasn't what she had prayed for.

"I'm sorry, Rachel, but your brother was taken prisoner," he said sadly when she reached him. "I'll do whatever I can but that might not be enough to save him. Captain Drusus is determined to make an example of the prisoners."

She stood no closer than five feet from Lucius. "You *must* free him, Lucius! He's only seventeen-years-old, for mercy sake. He's not a criminal, just a boy who longs to be free. He's no danger to Rome."

He took a step toward her, noticed her body grew ridged, and stopped. "I know that Rachel, but I have no authority to pardon anyone. All that I can do is try to persuade Captain Drusus to let him go."

She glared at him with eyes full of hate. "You can kill and punish, but not forgive. Is that your Roman utopia? If that's the empire you want us to be a part of then I hope we *never* give up our way of life!"

She started to cry as she turned away. Lucius watched her walk toward her house. He had little hope of being able to help Harim. He was convinced that she would always hate him.

Meanwhile, Rachel's family sat around the table talking about where Harim might be if he hadn't been arrested. When she came back from her conversation with Lucius she sat on a chair. "I just found out that Harim is in prison," she said bursting out in tears.

Sarah let out a scream and started crying. No one knew what to say until Elhanan asked, "Who told you that Harim is in prison?"

"Deborah told me that she read Harim's name of the list posted on the gate."

"I'll go talk with Captain Drusus," Elhanan said. "After all, he does know me and that I have been helpful. I'll promise him that Harim won't cause any more trouble."

Rachel's eyes opened wide, afraid her father would discover there were no names posted on the gate. "And risk losing you, too!" Sarah said. "No, Elhanan, you mustn't. It doesn't matter how helpful you were in the past. If Harim was with the Zealots and you tried to defend him Captain Drusus will think you might be one as well. No matter how much I love Harim, I'd die if you were crucified. Then who will take care of our family?"

"Mother's right, Father," Rachel said. "Please don't go."

Elhanan looked at Sarah, Rachel, Gideon and Jehoram. None of them were capable of taking over the responsibility for the family. He sighed. "You're right, Sarah. God forgive me, but I can't take the risk no matter how much I want to try to help Harim."

*   *   *

Lucius couldn't escape his deep feelings of remorse and guilt. *Of all the Romans in Galilee I had to be the man who arrested Rachel's brother. I alone am responsible for what happens to Harim, not Drusus or Caesar. And what happens to all revolutionaries is crucifixion. I knew that when I became a soldier. It doesn't matter one iota if Harim is only seventeen-years-old or if a lowly sergeant loves his sister.*

He racked his brain trying to think of something. Some scheme or reason to convince Drusus to set Harim free, but he couldn't think of anything. Then he did something he never did before in his life. He prayed. Oh, he had made all the religious sacrifices to his gods and performed meaningless rituals, but he never actually *prayed.*

Yet, when he tried to pray he knew that none of his gods could help. Still, he had to try. He called out to Jove, "O mighty Jove, hear me." Apart from calling out Jove's name, he wasn't able to say anything else. He realized that Jove didn't exist. Then he did the same with several other Roman gods, but again never got past their names. He fell to his knees in despair, covering his face with his hands.

Then inexplicably words came to his mind as if they were not really his. "God of Jesus, I don't know who you are but I believe that Jesus *does* know you! Please help me find a way to save Harim."

Not much later Lucius went to talk with Captain Drusus again about Harim. Drusus was in his quarters pacing back and forth dictating a letter to his scribe. Lucius paused at the door to wait until Drusus finished. Drusus noticed him, but ignored him as he continued his dictation. It became clear to Lucius that the letter was a report to Rome about the raid and the planned crucifixions of twenty-nine Jews.

When Drusus finished dictating he sat down and looked at Lucius with a suspicious scowl. "If you're here to try to persuade me not to execute the captives, Lucius, forget it!"

Lucius walked over to Drusus' desk and poured some wine without looking at Drusus. "Not at all," Lucius replied calmly, "you already convinced me that it's best to do that. However, one of my men told me that in the chaos of our attack a young boy was grabbed by mistake when he was nearby. The lad just happened to be in the wrong place at the wrong time. He wasn't actually a part of the Zealots. I suggest we let him go."

Lucius knew his lie *wasn't* God's answer to his prayer. "If he was near enough to be caught, so be it," Drusus replied. "I sentenced twenty-nine to die and we'll crucify all twenty-nine."

Lucius stared in silence at his captain who had been his friend for years, realizing it was hopeless. He knew that he couldn't change Drusus' mind any more than he could change who he was to please Rachel's mother. He stood and turned to walk away, but suddenly remembered one of the things he had heard Jesus say. "*Greater love hath no man than this, that he would lay down his life for a friend.*"

Is this the answer of Jesus' God? Lucius thought. *I don't love Harim but I do love his sister.* He realized he would never be happy without Rachel, and that she wouldn't forgive him if Harim were crucified. He didn't have the authority to free Harim, but he thought of one final way to try to bring about his release.

"You can still execute your twenty-nine men," Lucius said. "Let the boy go and crucify me instead."

Drusus jumped to his feet so abruptly he knocked over his chair. "What?" he shouted angrily. "You're crazy. Either that or you have been bewitched. You know how horrible it is to be crucified. You should, you've done it enough. You must be out of you're mind!"

"Maybe I am, but not in the sense that you mean. You're the one who sent me to spy on Jesus. Well, I believe what He said. Jesus taught that self-sacrifice for one's friend is the greatest expression of love there is."

"Listen here, Lucius, if you think you're playing some clever trick to force me into letting the boy go, forget it.

He'll die along with the others." Drusus was puzzled by Lucius' expression. "Who is this boy you're willing to give your life for?"

"The oldest son of Elhanan, Harim. You've met him when he came with his father to report the murder of one of our men. You also went to his home."

"I remember him, but you barely know this boy. He's hardly someone who could be considered a good enough friend to die for. Forget this nonsense and get out of here."

"True, I don't know Harim enough to die for, but I love his sister and I'm willing to die to make her happy."

"Your opinion of her love for you isn't very high if you think that *your* death in exchange for her brother's life would make her happy. Your death would accomplish nothing."

"I offer my life because I love her, not because she loves her brother more than me. Who knows, perhaps a hated Roman soldier's sacrifice for a Jew will change the way they think of us more than the executions of all the rebels who were arrested."

Drusus laughed. "You might be a fool, Lucius, but I'm not. The Jews wouldn't change their minds about us by such a stupid thing. Besides, I have no intention of allowing you to take Harim's place. I'll not sanction the crucifixion of a trained and experienced soldier under my command just so he can prove how much he loves a Jewish woman."

"It's my life, not yours! And it's my decision what I do with it, not yours!"

Drusus slapped Lucius hard in the face. "It's *not* your decision or your life. Your life belongs to Rome and you follow orders, not make decisions on your own. You ought to know that by now. Now get out of here before I have you flogged!"

Lucius couldn't even save Harim by offering his own life. He wondered why the God of Jesus hadn't answered his prayer. He turned and slowly walked out of Drusus' quarters like a wounded animal about to crawl off to die.

Chapter Eleven

That same night Rachel lay in bed emotionally exhausted from crying. She had wept for Harim and the rest of her family. Her grief mixed with hate for Lucius. She condemned herself in the privacy of her mind for having loved him. She covered her wet eyes with her arm, feeling ashamed. *How could I have been so blind for feeling anything but loathing for a man capable of killing innocent people? If only I had listened to my mother from the start.*

Like Lucius, she was haunted by something she remembered that Jesus had said. *"Forgive those that persecute you!"* They had sounded so wonderful when Jesus had said them, but that was before Harim had been arrested. Before Lucius had broken her heart.

How can I forgive such vicious cruelty? How could Lucius have said he agreed with Jesus and yet does such horrible things? She rolled over but her mind didn't rest. *How can I forgive myself for having loved him?* She eventually cried herself to sleep, asking that last question over and over again in her mind.

*   *   *

G. D. BALLEIN

Harim and twenty-eight other men were crucified outside the city two days later. Although Lucius didn't ask Drusus to remove him from the task, Drusus assigned the man under Lucius the responsibility of carrying it out. As was the case for all those who were crucified, friends and family were permitted to take down the bodies after they had hung on the cross in disgrace for the specified time.

Elhanan prohibited Gideon and Jehoram from going with Sarah and Rachel when he went to take Harim down from the cross. It was a horrible sight that made them sick to their stomachs. After they washed and rubbed his body in oil they wrapped him in linen before burying him. Then they wept as they staggered home.

For the next two weeks Lucius returned every day to where he and Rachel had met on the side of the hill overlooking the city and the sea. He hoped she might have softened in her hatred toward him, but wasn't surprised when she never came. He didn't expect her to forgive him. Finally, he reluctantly accepted the fact that she was no longer willing to be a part of his life, and stopped going to meet her.

Lucius tried hard to ignore his despair as he performed his duties as he always did in the past, but he had changed too much. He was gripped by guilt, his mind constantly echoing the words he had shared with Rachel about the glory of the Roman Empire. He desperately wanted to exorcise from his memory the scenes of past battles when he felt proud to be a soldier.

Adding to his shame was a recurring nightmare where soldiers swung their swords at young children. The children tried to run away as Rachel stood nearby, weeping and pointing her finger at him. He struggled in his nightmare to order the soldiers to stop the slaughter but was unable to speak. He looked at his right hand and saw that he was holding a decapitated head. With that, he usually woke up in a cold sweat.

140

By the time four months had past there was no longer any joy in Lucius' heart. He was dying inside as surely as if someone had pieced his heart with a sword. He despised himself, convinced he was no longer capable of caring about anyone or anything. He drank everyday until he was drunk in a vain attempt to forget Rachel. Drusus had been his friend for over six years, but now Lucius detested him. Drusus had rejected his every effort to release Harim. Yet, Lucius knew that Drusus was merely the focal point of his self-hatred.

Meanwhile, life in and around Capernaum appeared to have returned to normal. Fishermen were fishing, carpenters were building, tanners were drying skins and revolutionaries were scheming. However, beneath the surface more and more people were following Jesus.

Elhanan and Sarah couldn't afford to wallow in their grief. They had two other sons and a daughter to take care of. Like Lucius, they attended to their duties in spite of their sorrow. Yet, life didn't seem the same for any of them. Gideon went fishing with his father every day, and Rachel helped her mother around the house. One of them would say something about Harim on occasion, but found talking about him too painful. They eventually stopped mentioning his name.

One morning at breakfast Jehoram broke the informal code of silence. "I miss Harim. He always could make me laugh when I was sad."

Elhanan put his hand on Jehoram's hand. "We all miss him, Jehoram," he said, clearing his throat. "How would you like to go with me to ask Shemida to build a new chair for Martha's oldest son? He's getting old enough now to have a chair of his own. We'll go after Gideon and I get back from fishing."

"I'd like to do that."

Sarah was pleased Elhanan had thought of something to get Jehoram's mind off of Harim. She forced herself to smile, but it wasn't very convincing. "That's a marvelous idea,

Elhanan. That will make a splendid gift now that their family is growing."

Gideon looked at his father. "When you take Jehoram to Shemida's can I ask Ishbak and Elizabad to go with me to look for lost coins and weapons where the Egyptians fought the Romans?"

"That was over a hundred years ago, Gideon, but I don't see why not."

It wasn't a good day for fishing. The weather was calm on land, but the sea was rough. The water lapped hard against the side of the boat and the rocking of the boat made it unsafe to stand up to cast their net. After three hours Elhanan and Gideon went home.

Jehoram sat at the table building his temple. When he saw his father and Gideon walking toward the house he grabbed his crutch and went outside. "Are we going to Shemida's now?"

"After I salt our fish and drink some water," Elhanan answered.

Gideon turned to go to Ishbak's house when Sarah called out, "Wait a minute, Gideon. You're going to be gone for most of the day. I put together a basket of food for you and your friends. Just make sure you get back before it gets too dark."

Gideon took the basket. "Thanks, Mother. I won't be too late."

Ishbak, having finished his chores, sat under a palm tree eating a pear. He was glad to see Gideon walking toward him. "I'm going to where the Romans fought the Egyptians," Gideon said. "I'm going to look for coins and other stuff to sell. Do you want to come?"

"I sure do." Ishbak laughed, adding, "It sure sounds better than going to the garrison again. Let me ask my father if I can go."

Ishbak and Gideon walked to the back of the house where Ishbak's father made parchments out of papyrus. "I finished my chores, Father," Ishbak said. "Can I go with Gideon to look for coins where the Romans fought the Egyptians?"

"You can go, but you need to be back before dark. You better take some bread and cheese with you."

"My mother already gave me enough food for us," Gideon replied.

They said goodbye to Ishbak's father. "Let's ask Elizabad if he can come, too," Gideon said to Ishbak.

They ran to Elizabad's home to ask him to join them. After receiving permission from Elizabad's father the three friends headed for the battlefield located on a hillside almost an hour away. The prospects of finding something spurred them on with renewed vigor. When they reached the bottom of the hill they were surprised to see a massive crowd already gathering on the hillside.

"Look at that," Elizabad said. "I've never seen so many people before. It looks like the ground is slowly moving up the hill."

"They can't all be looking for coins!" Ishbak said.

They kept walking as more and more people arrived like ants on their way to a piece of bread on the ground. Halfway up the hill they turned around to see an incredible sight. Men, women and children were still coming by the hundreds.

"What's going on?" Elizabad asked. "Why are so many people coming here?"

Gideon, just as baffled, replied, "I don't know but whatever it is, it must be something important. Only the huge amphitheatre in Rome could hold such a large number of people. I imagine this is what it must look like when the Romans watch the gladiators."

Ishbak noticed a man with a familiar face standing on the peak of the hill. He shielded his eyes from the sun to study the man's face. Even from a distance he could tell from the expression on the man's face he was moved by the crowd. Then he pointed at the man. "I think that's the Rabbi, Jesus!"

"I don't want to disobey my father again," Gideon said. "He told me to stay away from Jesus. I think we should go home."

"Come on, Gideon, I don't want to go home now that we're here," Elizabad replied. "Let's at least wait to see what happens."

Gideon looked at his two friends who stared at him. "All right, but I don't like it."

The people, noticing Jesus standing on top of the hill, began to sit down as others still continued to arrive. After everyone was seated a strange silence covered the crowd. Then Jesus began to speak. He didn't shout but spoke normally in a calm, confident manner. Gideon and his two friends listened along with everyone else. Time itself seemed to stand still.

Jesus said, "If you have faith the size of mustard seed, you can say to this mountain, 'Move from here to there' and it will move. Nothing will be impossible."

Can that really be true? Gideon wondered.

By now the people, including Gideon and his friends, were hungry. A stranger walked up to them. "My name's Andrew," he said in a friendly tone. "I'm one of Jesus' followers. Would any of you happen to have some food?"

"I have a basket with two fish and five barley loaves for our meal," Gideon answered. "Why do you want to know?"

"May I have them?" Andrew answered, smiling broadly. "Jesus wants to feed these people. Some have come a long way, and it's been a long time since they have eaten. They are very hungry."

The three young friends glanced at each other at the incredible request. Gideon handed Andrew his basket. "Yes, but this won't be of much help."

"What's your name?" Andrew asked.

"Gideon, son of Elhanan."

"Thank you, Gideon, son of Elhanan."

As Andrew walked away with the food, Elizabad scoffed, "A lot of good our meager lunch will do for this crowd. What are we supposed to eat now that you gave away our food?"

"I'm sorry, Elizabad. I don't know why but I felt I should give Jesus our food."

They watched in fascination as a dozen men divided the crowd into groups of fifty. When that was accomplished the man Ishbak had identified as Jesus raised his hands in the air and blessed the food. The youngsters giggled at the unbelievable and foolish sight of twelve men walking among the people handing out food. They stopped laughing when they saw that the twelve men kept on passing out the food.

Ishbak scratched the top of his head. "They must have already had food before you gave them yours, Gideon."

"They couldn't have had that much food in their baskets," Gideon replied. "Besides, none of them has walked back to get more food. They keep handing out what they started with when they began."

Speechless now, they stared in astonishment at what was happening until everyone was eating, including them. Then the twelve followers of Jesus walked around to gather up the food that remained. Gideon remembered what Jesus had said about having faith the size of a mustard seed.

Gideon's eyes opened wide as he said in excitement, "Jesus *does* perform miracles! He *can* heal Jehoram!"

He jumped to his feet without saying another word to his startled friends. He ran home as fast as he could. When he barged into the house, Sarah, terrified that something horrible had happened, dropped a bowl of rice. He was so exhausted from running home he had to bend over to catch his breath, unable to speak.

She leaned over him and put her arms on his back. "Goodness, Gideon, you're all out of breath. What's happened?"

"Mother, I just saw Jesus perform an unbelievable miracle," he answered excitedly, gasping for breath. "He said that if you have faith the size of a mustard seed nothing is impossible. There must have been over a thousand people watching and listening to Him."

She breathed a sigh of relief and sat down. "Don't exaggerate, Gideon. Just what do you think you saw?"

"I'm *not* exaggerating mother. At least a thousand people were there! Honestly, there were that many people. When Ishbak, Elizabad and I saw this huge crowd sitting on the hillside we were curious as to what was going on. So we sat down to listen and watch. Jesus talked for a long time from on top of the hill. Anyway, after Jesus finished speaking a man came up to us and asked us if we had any food. He said he was a follower of Jesus and that Jesus wanted to feed the people."

"That's foolishness, Gideon, and I don't like it! Why in the world would anyone ask you for your food to feed as many as you claim were there? You know that such a crowd would require a whole wagon load of food."

"Please, Mother, let me tell you what happened. I gave the man the two fish and five barley loaves that you had given to me for our lunch. Then we saw a number of his followers divide the crowd into different groups. Jesus said a prayer for the food and then his followers handed it out. We watched them in disbelief. We were certain none of Jesus' followers had any other food. Jesus performed a miracle so everyone had something to eat!"

"You're must be mad from the sun. How can you believe such nonsense? Who do you think this rabbi is, Moses or Elijah? There hasn't been such a prophet for more than four hundred years. I don't want to hear another word about it!"

"Mother, please believe me. I *know* what I saw! When I first heard of Jesus I wanted father to take Jehoram to Jesus to see if He could heal him, but father and Harim persuaded me that I was wrong."

"Harim? You mean you had talked with him about Jesus?"

"Yes. Harim talked with several people about Jesus after I asked him what he thought. When they told Harim that Jesus was a dangerous fake, I gave up hoping that Jehoram could be healed. But now that I have seen Jesus perform a miracle I know that Jehoram *can* be healed."

Sarah was confounded that Gideon believed so strongly in what he had seen that he argued with her. "Listen, Gideon, I know how much you want Jehoram to be healed. No doubt that is why you have deluded yourself into believing such foolishness. Your father and Harim . . ." She chocked up when she mentioned Harim's name. She cleared her throat and added sadly, "Well, they knew what they were talking about."

"I'm not suggesting that I know more than they do, but I know what I saw. They passed judgement even though they never saw or heard Jesus. At least *ask* father to take Jehoram to Jesus. Isn't it worth taking a chance that I'm right?"

Elhanan and Jehoram walked into the house. "Not one more word in front of Jehoram," Sarah whispered in Gideon's ear. She smiled at Elhanan. "You were gone a long time just to ask Shemida to build a chair."

"I know," Elhanan replied. "I took Jehoram down to the sea to look for shells. He wants to crush them so he can decorate his temple, making it glisten in the sun." He looked at Gideon. "Did you find any coins?"

Gideon glanced at his mother. "No, I didn't."

* * *

Rather than being persuaded by Gideon's emotional appeal to take Jehoram to Jesus, Sarah worried that his obsession was a sign that he was in danger of losing his mind. She and Elhanan lay in bed that night looking at the stars through the window.

"I don't think Gideon's getting over Harim's death," Sarah whispered. "I'm frightened that he might be losing his mind."

"That's understandable," Elhanan replied, yawning. "He's always been very fond of Harim but hardly would lose his mind over it. Why do you think he is?"

"Gideon's convinced that he saw Jesus perform a miracle when he and his friends went looking for coins."

"You mean to tell me that Gideon disobeyed me again about listening to that heretic?"

"That's not important, Elhanan. What is important is his state of mind. He thinks he saw a miracle."

"What kind of miracle did Gideon say he saw?"

"It sounds ridiculous, but he's convinced that Jesus fed over a thousand people with his two fish and five barley loaves."

"That's nonsense. What did you tell him?"

"I told him that such a thing was impossible, but Gideon still insisted it was true."

"I was afraid Gideon's interest in this Jesus might cause trouble when he first spoke about him. I wish that Gideon had never heard about this Jesus."

"The fact is that Gideon not only has heard about Him, he actually thinks that Jesus can heal Jehoram. That's why I'm afraid that he's losing his senses. He even asked me to tell you to take Jehoram to Jesus to be healed."

"I'm not surprised. He asked me to do that when he first heard about Jesus, but I thought I had convinced him to give up on that idea. I frankly don't know what else to tell him. He's almost as stubborn as . . ." He was about to say *Harim* but stopped. Sarah knew what Elhanan was going to say.

They remained silent for a while until Elhanan said in resignation, "I'll talk with Gideon about it in the morning, although I doubt if it will do any good. On second thought, I'll talk with him on the boat when Jehoram isn't around. If

Jehoram overheard us talking about this foolishness it would build up his hopes for nothing."

"What about Rachel?" Sarah asked.

"What about Rachel?"

"I know she has gone to hear Jesus at least once. She hasn't talked to me about Him, but I think that she was favorably impressed with what He taught."

"Not Rachel, too. Well, we can't stop her from listening to Jesus, but you can at least tell her *not* to talk with Gideon or Jehoram about Jesus."

*   *   *

Elhanan and Gideon fished the next day on their boat as Elhanan said, "Your mother told me last night that you heard Jesus teaching when you were looking for coins. I must tell you, Gideon, that I was disappointed in you when I heard that. Even though I told you not to have anything to do with him, you disobeyed me."

Gideon wiped the sweat out of his eyes with the back of his hand and looked at his father. "I didn't mean to disobey you, Father. We didn't even know that Jesus was going to be there. We only went there to look for coins, but hundreds of people were already there. We were curious and wanted to know what was going on. Jesus began talking before we realized that it was Him."

Elhanan and Gideon tugged at the net full of fish. "Yet, you stayed to listen after you knew who it was. What's more, your mother told me that you thought you saw a miracle and wanted her to ask me to take Jehoram to see Jesus. Why did you ask your mother to do that after I had explained to you how these false Messiahs trick people by pretending to perform miracles?"

Gideon watched his father fling the net out into the sea. He realized that his father didn't believe Jesus had performed a miracle anymore than his mother had. Gideon knew it would be useless to try to convince his father that it had really happened. His heart sank, thinking, *Jehoram will never have the opportunity to be healed.*

When Gideon didn't say anything Elhanan glanced at him. He saw his young son staring out over the water, his sturdy shoulders slumped, his eyes full of tears. Elhanan shivered with guilt. Gideon looked exactly like he did when they heard about Harim's arrest.

Elhanan dropped the net in the boat and hugged Gideon tightly. "That's all right, son. I understand how you feel. I don't want you to stop praying that Jehoram will be healed some day. I just don't want you to be disappointed by trusting in some false Messiah."

Meanwhile, Sarah and Rachel washed clothes at a nearby stream. The stream wasn't very wide, but was knee-deep with plenty of smooth rocks along the edge that were excellent for their task. Sarah glanced at Rachel and asked, "Did you know that Gideon thought he witnessed a miracle yesterday when he and his friends heard Jesus?"

"No, I didn't know that. What did Gideon say Jesus did?"

"He said that Jesus fed over a thousand people with the two fish and five loaves of bread that I gave him."

Rachel had heard Jesus enough to think that He might have performed some miracle, but thought that such a thing was impossible. "Gideon must have been mistaken. There must have been food that Gideon didn't know was there. Besides, I heard Jesus at least seven times and there was never anywhere near that many people present."

Rachel immediately realized she shouldn't have mentioned she had heard Jesus more than once. *Mother might wonder how I heard Jesus that often when I told her I was going to Martha's.* "What did you tell Gideon?" Rachel asked.

"I told him that such a thing was impossible, naturally." Rachel breathed a sigh of relief when her mother asked, "What did you think about Jesus when you heard Him?"

Rachel sat back on her heels with her hands on her thighs. "Well, I liked most of what I've heard but not everything. I think He is a good man at heart but not very realistic." Rachel thought how much she hated Lucius. "For one thing, Jesus said that we should love those who hate us and forgive those who harm us."

Sarah stood up, picked up the basket full of clean clothes and put the basket on her head. "So our enemies can continue to harm us, no doubt. That isn't only unrealistic, it's stupid!"

Sarah turned to walk home. Rachel was up on her feet with another basket of wet items in her arms. "Listen, Rachel, you can think Jesus is a good man if you like, but I *don't* want you to encourage Gideon to believe in Him. And by all means, don't talk with Jehoram about miracles."

Rachel put her basket on her head. "I won't."

Chapter Twelve

Lucius continued to slip deeper and deeper into depression. Whenever Drusus or someone else spoke to him he would stare at them with a blank expression without saying a word, as if they weren't even there. Lucius obeyed Drusus' orders but did so silently and sullenly. He drank to excess, ate little and barely slept. No matter how hard his one time friend, Drusus, tried to break through to the man he had known—it failed to reach him. Drusus was convinced that Lucius was slowly but surely killing himself.

Early one morning Drusus saw Lucius kneeling in the dirt behind the stable spitting up blood. Drusus turned and walked away. He knew he *had* to do something or Lucius would die. He muttered under his breath, "What can I do? I've already tried everything I could think of, but nothing has worked."

Drusus felt desperate. Suddenly an idea came to Drusus. *I can't reach Lucius, but maybe there's someone else who can!* He went alone with fixed determination to where he had gone almost a year earlier. But this time it wasn't to see Elhanan.

When Sarah opened the door and saw the man she knew had sentenced Harim to death her eyes filled with hatred. So much hatred, she felt no fear. She glared at him and said in an angry voice, "If you looking for my husband, he isn't here."

Drusus wasn't surprised by her animosity. He hadn't expected otherwise, but he was there for Lucius sake, not to change the way they thought of him. "I'm not here to see your husband, but I do have information that your daughter would do well to hear."

His response alarmed Sarah greatly for her daughter's sake. As far as she knew Rachel hadn't done anything wrong. *What could he possibly want to say to Rachel?* Her hatred for Drusus boiled deep within her soul. She considered fabricating some reason why Rachel would have left Capernaum. At that precise instant she looked behind Drusus' back and noticed Rachel walking up the road toward them.

Rachel noticed a solitary soldier standing in front of her door. She assumed that it was Lucius. Tempted to turn around and walk away, Rachel decided it was best not to. She didn't want her mother to talk with Lucius by herself. She continued walking, preparing in the privacy of her mind the cutting words of hatred she would use to lash out at Lucius.

Drusus, hearing someone approaching behind him, turned to see whom it was. Rachel stopped dead in her tracks when she saw his face. *What would the man who had condemned my brother to death be doing here?* She glanced at her mother and saw the hatred in her eyes, but inexplicably, her mother didn't look frightened.

"Captain Drusus said he has something to tell you, Rachel."

"It was I who condemned Harim to death, not Sergeant Lucius." Drusus didn't sound apologetic. "In fact, Lucius offered his life in exchange for your brother."

Before Drusus could say more, Rachel said in a spiteful voice, "You're lying! Lucius didn't even know my brother."

"No, but he loves you."

Sarah glanced at Rachel in surprise. *When did he fall in love with Rachel?*

"Even so, why would he do such a thing?" Rachel asked.

"I asked Lucius why he was willing to give his life for your brother," Drusus replied. "Lucius told me that Jesus taught that giving up your life for another person was the greatest act of love there is. Personally, I thought that was pure madness and refused his foolish offer. Anyway, apparently Lucius believed Jesus. That's all I have to say. You can ignore it if you like, but I wanted you to know what happened."

Drusus walked away as Rachel thought, *I wonder why Drusus bothered to come here with his lie?*

Sarah walked into the house and sat down in front of the table. When Rachel came Sarah looked up at her. "So, you and this Sergeant Lucius must have been seeing each other all along. Don't try to lie about it, Rachel! How else could Lucius possibly have fallen in love with you?"

"We met and talked a number of times after I helped Martha. I thought I loved him but now I hate him." Rachel sat down and looked at her mother. "I'm sorry that I deceived you and father."

Sarah knew Rachel's heart was broken and didn't need a lecture. Her disappointment was no match for Rachel's sorrowful expression. She reached out and took Rachel's hand. "I'm sorry, too, Rachel. It's over and done with now, so let's not hear anymore about it."

They were both startled to hear Elhanan ask, as he stood in the doorway, "Hear about what?" He never saw Drusus when he left their house and was only mildly interested in what they were talking about. He walked in, went over to the sideboard to pour a glass of water from a jug, drank it straight down and joined them at the table.

Sarah, not having told her husband about Rachel's fascination with a Roman soldier, had no idea how he would take it when he found out that she had kept a secret from him. Rachel, sensing her mother's apprehension, answered for her.

"Captain Drusus came to tell me about a soldier that I have been seeing for some time. You met him when he accompanied you to where the dead soldier was found."

"You mean that you've been seeing Sergeant Lucius?" Elhanan asked. "When?"

"We met after I helped Martha with her children. It was Lucius who first told me that Harim had been arrested. He promised me that he'd try to have Harim released, but Captain Drusus refused."

"Then you lied when you told us that Deborah had seen Harim's name on a list of captives," Elhanan said in disappointment.

"Yes. I didn't want you to know that I had talked with Lucius."

Elhanan sighed, shaking his head. "I've never known you to lie to us before, Rachel."

"I never did. I'm sorry that I did this time."

"I don't understand why Captain Drusus came here to talk with you," Elhanan said.

"He came to tell me that Lucius had offered his life in exchange for Harim's." Rachel replied.

Rachel and her mother had thought the idea was ridiculous, but Elhanan didn't. He knew he would gladly give his life up for someone he loved. He leaned back and asked, "Did you believe what Drusus told you?"

"I'm not sure," Rachel answered. "I didn't at first but now I wonder if . . . I don't know."

"That wasn't what you had said when you accused Drusus of lying." Sarah snapped.

Rachel looked at her mother. "I know, but it just dawned on me that Drusus couldn't have known what Jesus had said if Lucius didn't tell him."

"I don't know what you mean," Elhanan replied. "What did Jesus say that Drusus couldn't have known?"

"Drusus had ordered Lucius to spy on Jesus because he was afraid he might cause trouble due to the large crowds following Him. That's when Lucius heard Jesus say that the greatest love is when a person gives up his life for his friend. Drusus would never have known Jesus said that if Lucius hadn't told him."

"How do you know all this?" Elhanan asked.

Rachel again looked at her mother. "Lucius had helped me about a year earlier, but we never met until we saw each other when we went to hear Jesus. The only time we saw each other after that was when we went to listen to Jesus."

Elhanan ran his hand through his long hair. "I see. Well, I don't know about Lucius, but I'd be willing to give my life for those I love."

Sarah remembered that Drusus had mentioned Jesus' words was the *reason* for Lucius' incredible offer. Her mind was a torrential storm of mixed emotions. She despised the Romans for killing Harim, was afraid that Rachel might forgive Lucius, and confused by her husband's lack of anger over the whole thing.

"Well, I *don't* believe it!" Sarah growled. "All I know is that Harim is dead and Lucius is still alive." She abruptly stood up and walked over to start to prepare their meal. She lowered her head in her hands, chocking back her tears. "Like I said earlier, it's over and I don't want to hear another word about it."

Rachel didn't say anything as she went over to help her mother prepare the meal. Elhanan sighed and went outside to find Gideon and Jehoram who had gone for a walk before Drusus had brought his disturbing message.

Later that evening Rachel went up on the roof to think about what Drusus had said about Lucius' offer to give his life. She paced back and forth under a cloudy sky. The more she thought about it, the more she realized that it must be true. Not only because of the depth of Lucius' love for her but also because Drusus wouldn't have had a reason to come and lie to her about it. Rachel felt miserable, struggling to convince herself that even if it *was* true she still hated Lucius.

It wasn't very long before her father joined her on the roof. By now a cool breeze began to blow her hair into her eyes. He walked over and put an arm around her waist as they looked out over the beloved city.

"Why didn't you ever tell me about seeing Lucius?" Elhanan asked sounding disappointed.

She looked at him with a solitary tear trickling down her cheek. "I was afraid that you would forbid me from seeing him. I'm so sorry that I have hurt mother and you so much."

He turned to face her and held her at arms' length, looking affectionately into her bloodshot eyes. "You know that we love you, Rachel. We both hoped someday you would marry a Jew. You and I know how your mother feels, but do you really think that I would expect you to deny your own feelings just to please me? However, your friendship with Lucius was *before* Harim was arrested. You must understand that now things are very different."

"Yes, I know that, Father. Anyhow, I no longer feel anything but hatred for Lucius."

Elhanan released her when she turned away to hide her tears. He had lived long enough to realize that love didn't die easily. He knew that no matter how much Rachel tried to convince herself she felt only hatred for Lucius, chances were that deep down she still loved him. He hoped that she *would* get over him, but that wasn't up to him. And if she didn't, he wanted her to know that he would be there.

"You're angry and hurt right now, Rachel," Elhanan replied, "but only time will tell how you'll feel in the future. If you ever feel that you need to talk about Lucius in the future come and talk with me. I promise you that I'll understand."

It started to rain and they went downstairs without saying anything more. That night marked the beginning of the rainy season.

*   *   *

There were two rainy seasons in this otherwise arid and hot land. One was in the spring and one in the fall. The seasonal rains were important to everyone who depended on them to fill the rivers and wells. It might rain off and on for a month or more. Sometimes it rained for days without stopping, causing mudslides.

This time it rained *hard* for nine consecutive days. Dark clouds covered the sky as the rain peppered the ground, the winds howling without mercy. The trees swayed violently and the sea bubbled with whitecaps as the rain blew sideways from a brutal wind.

People worried about what would happen to their homes if the deluge continued much longer. On the tenth day the rained finally stopped, but water continued to flow down slopes, resulting in mudslides that threatened trees and houses alike. Elhanan's family lived where it was safe, but many of their friends lived in places that were at risk. Caleb's house was one of them.

Elhanan and Gideon, like all the other fishermen, hadn't been able to fish for over a week. On the tenth day they decided to go fishing even though it was still cloudy and might start raining again. Rachel stayed home, but had visited Martha enough times to remember that a dry spring ran down the hill not far from their house. She was afraid the dry spring would make a natural spot for the rainwater to flow into, becoming a dangerous spring.

Rachel finished helping her mother around the house and sat across the table from her. She longed to ask her mother if she could go see how Martha was doing but couldn't bring herself to ask it. That had been the very ruse she had used as an excuse for seeing Lucius. Sarah knew from Rachel's expression that she was worried about something.

Sarah reached over and took a sandal out of Rachel's hand that she was going to repair. "I can do that, Rachel," Sarah said. "You go see how Martha and the children are doing." Rachel, astonished, looked at her mother who had a smile on her face. Sarah added, "Go on, Rachel. I know how worried you are about them."

Rachel jumped up and walked to the door where she stopped. She turned around to look at her mother. "Thank you, Mother," she said softly. "I won't be gone long."

When Rachel arrived at Martha's home she was alarmed to see that the swollen spring had already reached the backside of the house. She could tell the steady flow of water was slowly washing away the ground along the foundation. Rachel knew that if it continued it might eventually cause the wall to collapse. Rather than going in the house to see Martha, she immediately turned around and rushed back home.

Sarah was surprised Rachel had returned soaked in mud, trembling with concern. "Has their house been damaged?" Sarah asked anxiously.

"I don't think so but the water has reached the back of their house. I'm afraid that it might wash away the foundation."

"Well, for mercy sake, Rachel, go invite them to stay with us until the danger is past."

Rachel had planned on asking her if that was possible, but her mother, anticipating it, beat her to it. Rachel turned around to hurry back to Martha's without saying a word to her mother.

Martha was bathing her baby as Joshua played on the floor when Rachel knocked on the open door. Martha's face was that of a person who hadn't been sleeping well. "Come on in, Rachel, and pour us both a glass of wine," Martha said, lifting her baby out of the wood tub. "I just finished bathing the baby." Martha grabbed a towel and began drying off her baby. "How are things at your house?"

"We haven't had any problems due to the storm," she answered, pouring the wine. "I stopped by here a moment ago and noticed the water has reached the back of your house. When I told my mother about it she insisted that I ask your family to come stay with us until it's safe."

Martha looked at her, tears beginning to run down her cheeks. "Oh, thank you so much, Rachel! I've been worried sick about the children's safety sleeping in this place. You have no idea . . . how grateful . . . I am." She began to sob uncontrollably from the release of several days of stress.

Rachel went over and took the baby out of Martha's arms. "It's all right now, Martha! You will all be safe with us. Besides, it will give me the chance to be with your boys more." She kissed the baby on the cheek, and said with a large smile, "And you know how much I love that!" Rachel suddenly realized that Caleb wasn't home. "Has Caleb gone fishing?"

"No. He went to get stones and sand from the seaside to reinforce our foundation in back. I'll wait here until he comes home. He'll wonder where we are. I'll tell him that you invited us to stay at your house."

Joshua walked next to Rachel as she carried the baby to her house. When they got there Sarah smothered the baby in kisses. "Where's Martha?" she asked.

"She stayed home to tell Caleb they'll be staying with us for a while. Caleb has gone to the seashore to gather stones and sand to reinforce their foundation."

"Knowing your father, he'll want to go help Caleb when he gets home from fishing. It's a good thing I baked extra bread this morning. They'll be hungry after lifting stones and shoveling sand." She smiled at Rachel. "You've had plenty of time to watch Martha's boys, but now it's my chance. I'll watch them while you scrub the vegetables."

Elhanan was pleased when he and Gideon returned from fishing to learn that Sarah had thought of inviting Caleb's family to their home. "I'll go give Caleb a hand," he said.

Sarah and Rachel smiled at each other. "What did I tell you," Sarah mouthed silently.

"I'll go, too," Gideon said, heading out the door with his father.

For two days Rachel relished helping take care of Martha's sons while waiting for the water to subside from the back of Caleb's home. Jehoram enjoyed playing with the older son so much he said, "I wish they never would have to go back home."

Chapter Thirteen

Other than having their compound turned into a six-inch deep mud quagmire the Roman garrison didn't suffer any damage. The soldiers had to wear uncomfortable, stiff, rock-hard leather sandals that had been soaked by the wet, oozing mud. Drusus wasn't in a good mood when one of his men knocked on his open door.

"Sorry to disturb you, Captain, but there are four representatives from the city who would like to talk with you."

Drusus, sitting on his bunk, kicked a stool out of his way and walked over to sit behind his desk. "I prefer to sit here when talking with Jewish pests," he growled. "What the devil do they want now?"

"They didn't say."

"Well, tell them to take off their muddy sandals before coming in."

Drusus watched them in amusement through the open door as they leaned against each other for support to remove their sandals. When they entered Drusus' quarters a tall, plump man spoke in a baritone voice. "I'm Timnath, and these are three of my fellow elders of the Jewish council. We would like to ask you for a favor."

For someone wanting to ask a favor his tone sounded condescending, Drusus thought. Drusus leaned back in his chair, folded his arms in front of him and stared at Timnath. He didn't say anything as he looked down at their bare feet. He smiled, but remained mute. His four uninvited visitors grew increasingly apprehensive. Finally, Drusus asked in a harsh voice, "What sort of favor?"

"As you undoubtedly know, Captain Drusus, a good many of the houses along the hillside and at the bottom of the hill have been badly damaged by the effects of the storm. The owners came to us and said they're afraid their homes might collapse, but they don't want to leave them because of looters."

Drusus knew what they wanted but wasn't about to volunteer. "That's too bad, but what do you want me to do about it?"

"We'd like you to have some of your men patrol the area until the owners can go back home. We could have some of own people do it, but they would not be as . . ."

Timnath tried to find the right word. Drusus interrupted with a grin, "As *intimidating* as we would?"

Timnath's face turned red when he admitted, "Yes."

Drusus scratched his chin, enjoying the four barefooted men having to stoop so low as to request a favor from the detested Roman army. He replied in a sarcastic tone, "I see. You want *us* to protect your property." He was about to order them out when an idea occurred to him. *This might just be the thing to snap Lucius out of his self-hatred.* He leaned forward, elbows on his desk. "Well now, I certainly don't want looters running around loose, do I? I'll be happy to oblige your request." He laughed, adding as they turned to leave, "Don't forget to take your sandals."

As soon as they were gone Drusus looked at the soldier who stood at the door during the conversation. "Tell Lucius

I want to see him at once. I finally have something for him to do for the Jews that might please him. "

Lucius appeared in Drusus' doorway, his face gaunt and pale, his eyes bloodshot and his unwashed hair disheveled. He looked blankly at Drusus, but didn't say anything. He had lost at least fifteen pounds since he last saw Rachel, and his once firm muscles seemed to hang on his arms.

Drusus found looking at his friend difficult. He stared at his own folded hands that were on his desk as he spoke. "Four representatives from the Jewish council came to ask for our help. They want us to patrol the part of the city that was hit hardest by the storm and mudslides. I want you to be in charge of coordinating the patrols."

Drusus glanced at Lucius. The blank expression on Lucius' face hadn't changed, and he still hadn't said anything. He just stood there as if he were in a trance.

"Those miserable Jews hate our guts," Drusus growled, "but that never stops them from asking our help whenever they need it. Take as many men as you need with you."

Lucius didn't speak as he turned around and walked out. He saw of one of his men banging one of his sandals against a post to reduce its stiffness. He walked over and said, "Pick out twenty men and tell them that I want them to meet me at the gate in ten minutes."

When they were all assembled at the gate, Lucius divided them into five groups of four men in each group. Then he said, "I want one group to patrol the hill and lower part of the city for five hours. Then come back here so another group can take your place. That will take twenty-five hours for all five groups to patrol the area. Then we'll start all over again. You're to keep doing this until I say otherwise. You are to be looking for looters, and that's *all* you're looking for. Antonias, you're in charge. I want you to assign when each group is to go, and I want you to make sure they do it. I'll go with the first group."

On the second day of the patrol Lucius and four of his men made their way up one of the roads on the hillside just a large cypress tree suddenly crashed down on top of a house fifty yards in front of them. They heard a woman scream.

"Come with me!" Lucius yelled. He charged up the hill, his men following behind him. When Lucius got there a woman staggered out of the badly damaged house screaming hysterically with her three-year-old daughter in her arms. She put down her daughter on the ground and turned around to go back into the house.

Lucius grabbed her arm. "Stop, you can't go back in there! Can't you see that the wall is about to collapse?"

She tried to break loose, shrieking in terror. "Let me go! My husband and baby are still in there!"

The huge tree rolled over several feet causing the house to groan from the weight. Lucius realized it indicated the wall was giving way. Lucius looked at one of his men. "Marcus, hold onto her while I go in!" Months of self-hatred and listlessness that had enslaved Lucius were suddenly gone.

Marcus held her tight as he objected in an anxious voice, "You can't go in there, Sergeant! That wall is about to give way any minute."

Lucius, ignoring the warning, pushed some debris out of the way so he could go in. Another soldier attempted to restrain him, but Lucius jerked his arm away. "I'll not stand here and let a baby die without trying to save it!" he snapped angrily.

Lucius squeezed through the small opening as the wall creaked under the weight of the tree. Once inside the house he saw the father pinned beneath a heavy piece of interior wall that had collapsed. The father was conscious, but couldn't free his legs. Lucius glanced quickly around the room looking for something to use as a lever. He noticed a crushed table, and heard the sound of the baby crying in another room. He broke off one of the table's legs to use as a fulcrum in order to pry up the wall.

G. D. BALLEIN

Lucius, straining to lift the wall so the father could crawl out, lifted it a few inches. "Try to move now," he said with a groan.

The father slid one leg out, moaning in pain. "I can't get my other leg out."

Lucius took a deep breath and used every ounce of strength he had to lift the wall a bit higher. The father twisted his leg, and gasped, "I'm free."

A handful of neighbors, who had heard the sound of the tree falling and subsequent screams of the mother, rushed to the scene to help. By the time they got there Lucius was already in the house. Seeing the mother and three-year-old, but not the father or baby, they realized they must be trapped in the house.

"Let's get them out of there," one cried moving toward the house.

"Don't move anything!" Marcus shouted. "Our sergeant is already in the house trying to rescue the father and baby."

They couldn't believe their ears. A Roman soldier was actually risking his life to save some Jews. Inside the house, Lucius said to the father, "The fact that your baby is still crying means that he's still alive."

Lucius and the father worked together with as much care as they could to clear a tiny passageway without making more debris fall. The father looked through a small opening into the room where the baby was trapped, but couldn't see him. Small chunks of the roof started to fall onto them like raindrops as the wall continued to moan. It was an ominous sound.

"We better work faster," Lucius said.

After a few minutes they made a small opening into the baby's room. The father was too big to fit through the tiny gap, but Lucius managed to squeeze through. When he was halfway through he saw the baby. "I can see the baby!" he yelled excitedly.

Lucius crawled the rest of the way through, picked up the baby and shouted to the father, "I'll hand him out to you through the hole. You better get him out of here fast!"

The father grabbed his baby, and limped out of the house on his injured leg as fast as he could. The witnesses cheered but suddenly stopped when the tree shifted once more, enabling the wall to finally collapse into a cloud of dust. There was nothing left standing. The horrified soldiers and Jewish neighbors frantically removed the debris in faint hopes that Lucius might have somehow survived.

They assumed the worst when they heard no sounds coming from underneath the ruins of what had been a house. Fifteen minutes later they found an unconscious and badly injured Lucius. The back of his head was already caked in dried blood, and his right shoulder crushed. The panicky soldiers carried him back to their garrison as the astonished neighbors watched. They couldn't believe such compassion by a Roman soldier.

The soldiers carried Lucius into his quarters and lay him on his bunk. Gnaeus said, "Go get the doctor, Marcus. I'll go tell Drusus what happened."

Drusus sat at his table eating figs when Gnaeus barged in, gasping for breath. "Sergeant Lucius was badly injured when he crawled into a house to save a baby."

"What!" Drusus yelled, jumping off his chair. "Where is he?"

"In his quarters. Marcus already went to get the doctor."

Drusus rushed to Lucius' quarters as fast as possible. Lucius was unconscious, dried blood on his forehead and left cheek. Drusus stood at the head of Lucius' cot with his arms folded in front of him, watching the doctor wash the blood from the back of Lucius' head.

"He has a severe gash on the back of his head, but his skull isn't broken," the doctor muttered to himself. Then he ran his hand along Lucius' ribcage, and said too callously for Drusus to appreciate, "At least two of his ribs on his right side are broken." Rolling Lucius over on his right side, the doctor noticed that his red shirt felt tacky. He looked at his hand and grimaced as he said, "Blood! Something pierced him in the back pretty deep, but I can't tell if it hit any vital organ." Finally, he examined Lucius' right shoulder. "Whatever hit him here had to be very heavy to shatter the bone this much."

The physician stood up and looked at Drusus. "Whether or not he lives or dies all depends upon if the wound to his back did any damaged to an internal organ." He wiped the blood off his hands onto a piece of cloth. "Either way, I'm sure that his right arm will never be very strong again."

Drusus looked down at his unconscious friend. He shook his head, mumbling to himself, "It seems that you were determined to give your life for a Jew after all, weren't you my old friend?"

Over the next several days there was little improvement in Lucius' condition, although on the second day they managed to get a slight amount of warm broth inside him before he passed out. Early on the morning of the third day, Lucius regained consciousness long enough to see that Drusus had come to see how he was doing. Lucius closed his tired eyes as he tried to speak. He winced from the pain when he reached for his injured shoulder.

Lucius opened his eyes, motioning for Drusus to bend down. "Did the father . . . get his baby . . . out in time?" he asked in little more that a whisper.

Drusus had no idea, and glanced at one of the soldiers who had been there. He nodded, and Drusus answered in a quiet voice, "Yes, he did, thanks to you." Drusus was disappointment when Lucius passed out again. He realized that Lucius, having no fight left in him, was content to die now that he knew the baby was safe.

Drusus put his hand on Lucius' knee. "Well, my old friend, I'm not content to let you die without trying once more to give you a reason to live."

Drusus marched out of Lucius' room and headed straight for Rachel's house. *Let's just see if a Jew is as willing to save Lucius' stubborn hide, as he was to risk his life for one of them.*

When Drusus got there Rachel was outside beating a wool blanket hanging over the washing line with a stick. Rachel sighed when Drusus walked toward her. "Why can't you just leave us alone?" she said under her breath.

Elhanan and Gideon watched and listened in silence to what Drusus had to say. Drusus, ignoring them, spoke directly to Rachel. "You might not have believed me when I came here to tell you that Lucius offered his life for your brother. I can't blame you if you didn't. Now believe this! Lucius lies near death at our garrison for having saved a Jewish father and his baby three days ago."

Rachel, stunned, gasped and covered her mouth. Without looking at her father, she asked Drusus, "Can I come and see him?"

"That's precisely how I hoped you would respond," Drusus answered with a broad smile. "Why else would I have come here to tell you about it?"

Elhanan stepped forward and took Rachel's hand in his. "I'll go with you, Rachel." Rachel wiped a tear from her eye with the back of her other hand as Elhanan looked at Gideon. "Go in the house and tell your mother what Captain Drusus said. Tell her that I'm going with Rachel to the garrison. We'll have to go fishing when I get back. In the meantime, you can do something with Jehoram."

The pleased expression of Drusus' face made it clear that he approved of Elhanan's decision. Rachel did even more so. She squeezed her father's hand for support the entire time it took to walk to the garrison. People couldn't help but stare at the unusual sight of the unlikely trio walking together like lifelong friends.

Gideon went into the house and said, "Captain Drusus was outside. He came to tell Rachel that Lucius is dying. He told Rachel that Lucius had saved a father and baby. Rachel and father are going with Captain Drusus to the garrison to see him."

Sarah sat down with a deep sigh. There was no doubt in her mind that Rachel still cared about Lucius, and she wasn't happy about it. Caleb had a different reaction altogether. He had heard about a soldier who had saved a Jewish father and baby, but only now knew *who* that soldier was. *So that's who it was. I remember Lucius' name from when Rachel asked me to go to the garrison to deliver her message to him.*

Sarah, Gideon and Jehoram hugged Martha's children to say goodbye, and Caleb's family headed home. As soon as they walked out of the house, Caleb stopped and looked at Martha. "I've got something important to do. Take the children home and I'll be there as soon as I can."

Caleb kissed Martha and his children, and quickly headed for the same neighborhood where Lucius had rescued the father and baby. When he got there he talked with the neighbors about the accident. He had something on his mind besides idle curiosity.

*   *   *

It didn't take long for Drusus, Rachel and Elhanan to reach the garrison. Rachel, having never been inside the garrison before, thought, *What a dismal place.* Drusus led them into the stuffy, dim room where Lucius lay unconscious on a cot. Rachel froze in her tracks just inside the room, and stared across the room at Lucius. She felt worried and nervous.

Elhanan leaned forward to whisper in her ear. "It's all right, Rachel. You go over and talk with him even though it seems he can't hear you." She took two steps, stopped and looked back at her father. "Go on, Rachel. Tell him how you feel."

Rachel looked at her father in astonishment, tears flowing down her cheeks. Elhanan smiled and repeated, "Yes, Rachel. Tell him *exactly* how you feel."

Rachel walked over to kneel beside Lucius' cot. She gently pushed the hair off his forehead, and stared at him before trying to speak. She wiped her eyes, and sniffed. She thought he looked dead. He face was white and he was barely breathing.

Rachel took a deep breath, and whispered, "Lucius, this is Rachel. Can you hear me?"

When there was no response she looked at her father and Drusus standing by the doorway. Drusus waved his hand in a small circle a few times indicating that she should continue talking. Rachel touched Lucius' cheek tenderly. "It's Rachel. Please tell me that you can hear me."

Lucius still showed no sign of waking up from his deathlike slumber. She took his left hand in hers and held it to her neck, softly pleading over and over for him to wake up. Elhanan and Drusus stood by the door, silently watching and listening to Rachel's pleas.

Then in her despair she pleaded with someone else. "Please God, let him live!"

She sat by his side for half an hour without speaking. Then she stood up, touched his cheek once more and walked over to her father and Drusus. She looked at Drusus, but really asked her father as well, "May we take him to our house and watch over him?"

They were both surprised by her request, but before either could answer a weak voice behind her muttered softly, "Rachel?"

She rushed back to the cot and grabbed his hand. "Yes Lucius, its Rachel! I'm here right beside you."

Lucius opened his eyes for a brief moment, smiled and closed his eyes. "I thought I was dreaming . . . when I heard your voice."

She squeezed his hand, choking back the tears. "It wasn't a dream my love. I'm really here! I'm here right next to you."

His tried to open his eyes again, but couldn't. He barely was able to whisper, "Please forgive . . . me, Rachel, for not being . . . able to save your brother. You were . . . right after all. I can kill . . . but not . . ." He passed out before he could finish.

Rachel either didn't realize that he was unconscious or hoped that he could hear her anyway when she replied, "I know you tried. I know, I know. Captain Drusus told me that you offered your life for Harim. I forgive you, and beg you to forgive me for all the hateful things I said to you."

Rachel continued to hold his hand, staring at his seemingly lifeless face while Drusus and Elhanan quietly talked about Rachel's request. "I understand your daughter's wish to take care of Lucius at your home, but I think he should stay here," Drusus whispered. "We have a doctor who knows how to take care of such wounds. Besides, your family would be in an awkward position if your neighbors knew you were taking care of a Roman soldier in your home."

Elhanan glanced at Rachel sitting next to Lucius. He knew how much Rachel wanted to take care of Lucius, but knew Drusus was right. "I agree, although I know Rachel will be disappointed. It will also give me time to try to persuade my wife to accept the fact that they will never change how they feel about each other. No offense intended, but you probably know that Jews don't marry non-Jews without causing a great deal of opposition within their families."

"Yes, I know that, even though I've never been able to understand it. I take it that your wife feels more strongly about that than you do."

"Not really, no. Let's just say that I'm more realistic and willing to accept the inevitable." Elhanan looked at Rachel. "Rachel loves and respects us, but she will want to marry Lucius no matter what we say."

Rachel finally realized Lucius wasn't going to wake up. She kissed Lucius on the forehead, and joined Drusus and her father. Drusus took full responsibility for their decision. "I'm sorry, Rachel, but I've decided that Lucius needs to stay here until he's recovered. However, I think it would help him if you could visit him as often as you can. I'll have one of my men escort you to and from your home, if you would like."

Rachel was disappointed but didn't protest Drusus' decision. "Thank you, but I don't think that will be necessary."

"I understand, Rachel," Drusus replied. "It would be better if people didn't see you walking back and forth to the garrison with a soldier."

Rachel glanced back at Lucius, hating to leave. "I'll come back every day if my mother says that I may." Then she walked back to kiss Lucius on the forehead again.

On their way home Rachel thought about how her mother would react. "Tell me Father, what do you think I should say to mother? I know that she will be very unhappy."

"I've already been thinking about that very thing." He took her hand in his and smiled. "Well, assuming that you and Lucius *won't* give each other up, the ideal situation would be if Lucius was willing to convert to Judaism. But even that might not be enough for your mother. Even though Lucius tried to save Harim and did convert to our faith, he still would be a Roman soldier. Soldiers can't simply quit when they want."

Elhanan stopped walking and looked deep into her eyes, aware that Rachel would hate what he was about to say. "There's only one thing I can think of that you and Drusus can do. Accept the possibility that your mother might never want to see you again. If that happens, it might be easier on both of you in the long run if you and Lucius moved out of the area. Perhaps out of Galilee altogether."

Rachel's face turned white from shock. She jerked her hand away and stared at her father in disbelief. "What? How can you suggest such a terrible thing? I couldn't live without seeing all of you!"

Elhanan, having anticipated her reaction, took her hand again. "Listen, Rachel, I understand how much that hurts you. It grieves me to even suggest it, but you must face the truth. Surely you realize how painful it would be if you stayed here when you *couldn't* see your mother."

Rachel's heart ached and her mind raced wildly as she thought about choosing between Lucius and her family. She looked at her father, tears pouring down her cheeks. "It's not fair to have to choose between you and Lucius. How could I stand such a miserable and lonely life?"

Tears came to Elhanan's eyes as he answered sadly, "By making a new life with your husband, that's how. You know the Scripture teaches that a man or a woman must be willing to leave their family to be with their wife or husband. God's word isn't naïve or simplistic, Rachel. It deals with life's situations honestly and realistically. We might not always like it or want to abide by its teaching, but it is *always* right. It might not seem like it now, Rachel, but God's word is best for everyone who believes in it in the end."

"That's odd that you would say that, Father. I remember Jesus once said that '*God's Word is Truth*' when a Sadducee accused Him of blasphemy."

"Did Jesus actually say that?"

"Yes, He did. Jesus often quoted the Scriptures when He taught. That's why I was so shocked when some of our religious leaders hate Him so much."

For the first time Elhanan questioned in his own mind *why* he had been so adamant in his rejection of Jesus. *I've never heard or seen Jesus, yet I dismissed Gideon and Rachel's opinion of Jesus without hesitation. True, Rabbi Jacobs had denounced Jesus as a heretic and blasphemer, but based upon what? Certainly not upon what Gideon and Rachel told me Jesus taught. No, no. It wasn't because of what Jesus supposedly said. It was because of the preposterous notion that Jesus could perform miracles.*

Chapter Fourteen

When they reached home Sarah glared at Elhanan and Rachel while setting the table for supper. Elhanan, knowing how she felt, sat down in his usual seat. Rachel immediately began to help her mother. The silence was deafening. No one seemed to notice that Jehoram and Gideon weren't there.

Suddenly, Jehoram hobbled into the kitchen with Gideon laughing right behind him. Oblivious of the morgue-like atmosphere, Jehoram boasted, "I told you that I could beat you if you hopped on one foot from the olive tree."

Gideon bobbed Jehoram gently on the top of his head as he sat down, laughing. "That's only because I fell three times. Just wait until next time. I'll leave you in the dust."

Jehoram and Gideon's antics broke the sullen atmosphere, causing Sarah to smile as she rebuked her sons. "If you two rambunctious characters are quite finished disrupting the whole city, your father is ready to say the blessing for our meal."

They held hands are usual as Elhanan prayed. "Blessed art Thou, O Lord! King of the universe! Who provides us with bread from the earth." Then he smiled at Gideon. "Well, what mischief did you and Jehoram get into today?"

Gideon fixed his eyes on his plate in front of him and put his hands on his lap, his face turning red with guilt. "Forgive me for doing something that you told me not to do," Gideon answered.

Not Gideon, too! Elhanan thought. *I had one son who insisted on associating with Zealots, a daughter who fell in love with a soldier, and now an eleven-year-old who admitted he disobeyed me.* He sighed and asked, "Why, what did you do?"

"Jehoram and I went for a walk near the synagogue. I had no idea that Jesus would be there, but we stayed and listened to Him."

Elhanan leaned back in his chair, shaking his head in frustration. "What, again? Why is it, Gideon, that you seem to run into Jesus every time you leave the house?" His tone wasn't nearly as harsh as it has been before when he scolded Gideon about listening to Jesus. He remembered that a few minutes earlier he also wondered about Jesus. He smiled as he looked at Jehoram. "Well, Jehoram, both Rachel and Gideon approve of Jesus. Now that you've heard Jesus, what's your opinion of Him?"

Jehoram, thrilled his father wanted to know his opinion, blurted out cheerfully, "I liked Him!"

Elhanan looked at his wife with a sly grin. "It's unanimous. It appears that all three of our children like Jesus. Evidently Jesus has a special appeal to Jewish children."

Rachel looked at her father, and put her hand on Gideon's shoulder. "Not just children, Father, and not just Jews." She looked anxiously at her mother for a moment and took a deep breath. "Lucius isn't a child or a Jew, and yet he agreed with Jesus every time he heard Him speak."

Sarah stared at Rachel in disbelief, assuming Rachel was trying to make Lucius look less Roman. Elhanan leaned forward to ask Rachel, "How do you know that? When did Lucius hear Jesus?"

"I told you earlier that Lucius was ordered by Captain Drusus to spy on Jesus because Drusus was concerned about the large crowd of Jews who were attracted to Jesus. Lucius heard Jesus three times before we met and five times after that. When I asked Lucius what he thought about Jesus he told me that he agreed with everything He said."

Sarah said under her breath, "I wonder if Drusus told us the truth when he said Lucius had offered his life for Harim because of something Jesus had taught?" Her tone reflected her bewilderment. *Could I have been wrong about Lucius?*

Elhanan looked at his wife's soft eyes, and was puzzled by what he saw. *Is it possible Sarah's changing her feelings about Lucius?* Elhanan stood up, and began pacing back and forth as his baffled family watched his enigmatic action. They knew something troubled him. *If Sarah is willing to change her mind about Lucius, maybe I was wrong about Jesus? No! No! No! Jesus might impress people with His words, but miracles are not possible!*

Elhanan was about to sit down to declare his judgment on Jesus once and for all when he looked out his front door and saw a frightening sight. A dozen Jewish men were walking straight for his house. Elhanan assumed they had heard about Rachel and the trip to the garrison to visit a wounded soldier, and were coming to warn them to have nothing to do with the Romans.

He glanced at Rachel, feeling afraid for her safety. He wanted to warn her of the impending trouble that her love for Lucius was producing, but couldn't do it. Not in front of Sarah. Besides, he knew Rachel would find that out when the men marching toward their house threatened her. Sarah saw the alarmed look on Elhanan's face. He walked out the door as Sarah got up to join him at the door. Rachel and Gideon followed right behind.

Elhanan was hurt when he noticed that Caleb was one of the men in front. The men stopped ten feet in front of the house. Caleb stepped forward with a large smile on his face. He said in a loud, proud voice, "Elhanan, you see here some of the men who were there when Lucius risked his life to save Jonathan and his baby. These men helped dig Lucius out of the debris when the wall fell on him. Although they didn't know who he was, they knew a Roman soldier had almost been killed trying to save a family of Jews for no other reason than for compassion."

Elhanan, dumbfounded, replied, "I don't understand. I'm surprised that you came here to tell me that."

Caleb laughed. "I'm not surprised that you *are* surprised! You and your family showed me the same kind of compassion when you invited my family into your home. When I heard that Rachel's friend, Lucius, was the one who had been injured I knew that you might need some friends of your own. You see here, Elhanan, some of your *Jewish* friends. Like I said, they *saw* what kind of man Lucius is. We've come to pledge our support for your friendship with a Roman soldier by the name of Lucius."

Elhanan's whole family was overwhelmed. A tear came to Elhanan eye as he walked over to hug each man. When he finished he looked at them and tried to speak, but couldn't. He cleared his throat and said simply, "*Shalom!*"

Elhanan's family watched them walk away. When they were out of sight Elhanan's family went back into the house. They sat around the table, still amazed at what happened. No one said anything for a while, until Elhanan spoke. "I think we just experienced a miracle. Imagine, Jews pledging their support for us so we can be friends with a Roman soldier. I never imagined I'd ever lived to see such a wondrous thing."

Elhanan glanced at Gideon and felt ashamed. He lowered his head, sniffed and cleared his throat. "I'm sorry that I didn't believe you when you told us Jesus fed the crowd with your lunch, Gideon. I've been wrong in telling you there are no miracles. God does work in wondrous ways. We just experienced it."

Elhanan cleared his throat again, looked at his wife and then Rachel. Finally, he looked at Jehoram with a tear in his eye. "There are all kinds of miracles, Jehoram. I'm sorry it has taken so long to discover that. Your brother, Gideon, had more faith than any of us. I now believe God does heal the deep-seated hatred between people, the broken heart and the spirit. There's no greater miracle than that. I also believe God can heal the body."

Elhanan reached out his long arms and put them around Gideon and Jehoram. He closed his moist eyes, praying softly, "God forgive me for doubting your mercy and power. And thank you for my family who have trusted and believed in you all along." He opened his eyes to look at Gideon with a large smile. "You never gave up on Jesus. Find out when and where Jesus is speaking next. We'll take Jehoram to see Him."

*   *   *

Jesus had gone to the other side of the Sea of Galilee for four days. During that time Elhanan and Gideon went fishing leaving Sarah and Rachel to discuss Rachel's future. The day after Caleb and his friends visited Elhanan with their pledge of support, Rachel went to visit Lucius after she had finished her chores. He was still very weak, but was improving. He tried to sit up, only to fall back on his pillow.

Rachel sat by his cot to feed him small slices of melon, apples and pears. "You'll never believe what happened," she said. "Do you remember the man who took my letter to you?" Lucius nodded. "His name is Caleb," Rachel said. "He came to our house with a number of Jewish friends to pledge their support of our friendship."

"Did they really? What brought that about?"

"You did," she answered, pushing a slice of apple in his mouth. "They saw you when you rescued Jonathan and his baby. Anyway, my father was so moved by their action that he told Jehoram he would take him to see Jesus to be healed."

Lucius, delighted to be near Rachel, smiled with each word Rachel said in her sweet, soft voice. "I wish I could go with them," he said.

Rachel touched Lucius on the cheek. "When I heard about what had happened to you, I came here with my father but you were unconscious most of the time. You woke up long enough to ask me to forgive you, and then passed out again. Do you remember that?"

"I vaguely recall that, yes."

"Well, I said that I *did* forgive you. Then I asked you to forgive me, but you were not able to hear me."

He looked at her with deep affection. "I have nothing to forgive, Rachel. You had every reason in the world to despise me. I let you down when you needed me. Your brother wouldn't have died if it wasn't for me."

Rachel put the last apple slice in his mouth, and leaned forward to kiss his forehead. "Drusus told me that you offered your life for Harim's freedom. You did all you could to help him, Lucius. Please don't punish yourself over Harim's death. Not even mother or father blames you for that anymore. Harim died because he didn't listen to my father's advice. Now, would you like some slices of pear?"

"Yes, please." When she went to put a slice of pear in his mouth he took her hand and kissed it. "I want to tell you some wonderful news before you go. I'm no longer a soldier."

"What are you talking about? You just can't quit being a Roman soldier. You wouldn't be allowed. They will arrest you if you tried to leave."

"There are many things that you don't know about being a Roman soldier, Rachel. Soldiers need *two* strong arms not just one. Ordinarily a soldier is expected to serve for twenty years *unless* they can no longer fight. The doctor said that I might have some use of my right arm, but not enough for a soldier."

Tears of joy ran down Rachel's cheeks, but she could tell Lucius was exhausted. She leaned forward and kissed him on the mouth. "I better go now to let you get some rest, but I'll be back tomorrow." She smiled when she stood up to leave, but he never saw it. His tired eyes had closed and he immediately fell asleep. She whispered, "I love you, Lucius."

When Rachel turned toward the door she saw Drusus standing mute in front of it. She walked toward him and asked, "Is it true that a soldier with a bad arm can quit?"

He smiled slyly. "Not exactly, no. There are a number of other duties that a man can do besides fight. Cook or take care of the horses. You know, that sort of thing."

Rachel nodded and smiled. "That's what I thought. You lied to Lucius about that, didn't you?"

They walked out together as Drusus answered, "Yes, as a matter of fact I did happen to mention that." He stopped walking and looked into her eyes. "I'm sorry, Rachel, that I didn't pardon your brother." He sounded remorseful and looked ashamed. "Lucius tried to tell me that mercy would do more to bring peace to Galilee than force, but I didn't believe it. Now I realize that Lucius was right. I can't bring your brother back but at least I can let you have Lucius."

Rachel looked at the man she had hated so much and remembered the words of her father to Jehoram. "*God heals the hatred between people and the broken heart.*" Drusus started to walk away, but Rachel flung her arms around his neck. "Thank you, Drusus. You've made me very happy."

He gently pulled her arms away and said softly, "Do me a favor, Rachel. Don't tell Lucius that I lied until you're both old and gray with children of your own. Then one day while walking under the stars tell him how gullible he was to have believed his old friend."

Rachel wiped a single tear from her eye. "I promise!"

When Rachel arrived home her mother was churning the wheel making cheese. "How was Lucius today?" Sarah asked. "I hope he was able to eat the fruit you took with you."

Rachel relieved her mother behind the wheel. "Yes, he ate everything but the melon. He still is very weak but is getting stronger every day."

"I'll not lie to you about my wish that you wouldn't get married, but I love you and pray that you'll be happy. If I can't give you my wholehearted approval, I'll certainly give you my blessing. Although a number of our friends have pledged their continued friendship, there will be many others who will despise you. What's more, I don't even know if soldiers are permitted to get married."

"Lucius isn't a soldier anymore. Drusus told him that a soldier with a bad arm could be released from the army." Rachel looked at her mother, wondering if she should tell her that Drusus had lied. She decided to respect Drusus' wish to keep it a secret.

* * *

When Elhanan and Gideon came home from fishing Gideon ran into the house thirty yards ahead of his father. "Where's Jehoram?" he yelled excitedly.

Jehoram, who was seated at the table right in front of Gideon, answered, "I'm down by the seashore looking for you."

Sarah and Rachel wondered what in the world had gotten into Gideon to make him so excited. They had their answer when Gideon announced, "Jesus is back from the other side of the sea. He's only half a mile from here. Father said we're going to take Jehoram to see Him!"

Elhanan walked in and teased, "I heard Gideon screaming for all the world to hear that Jesus is here." He picked up Jehoram and swung him around onto his back. He looked at Sarah and Rachel. His smile was contagious. "Let's go before Gideon goes without us."

When they arrived on the same hillside where Jesus had preached and healed others on other occasions a large crowd was already there. Elhanan's heart sank. "How can we possibly reach Jesus so He can heal Jehoram?"

"Don't worry, Father, Jesus will heal Jehoram," Gideon answered.

The crowd wasn't a mob. People were patient as they watched and listened to Jesus. "Come to me, all who are weary and burdened, and I will give you rest. Take my yoke

182

upon you and learn from me, for I am gentle and humble in heart, and you will find rest for your souls. For my yoke is easy and my burden is light."

Jesus walked among the people knowing those who had faith in Him. Jesus looked at the crowd and raised his arms. "I tell you the truth, if you have faith as small as a mustard seed, you can say to this mountain, 'Move from here to there' and it will move. Nothing will be impossible for you."

Jesus spoke to all who would listen, touching the blind, deaf, sick and lame. He walked up to Gideon and smiled. "I know that it was your faith that brought your family here today. Be of good cheer, Gideon. Your brother is healed."

Most of the people were amazed by what Jesus did. The Pharisees were angry, not amazed. They left, determined to kill Him.

As Elhanan's family drew near their home, Jehoram said, "I'll race you home, Gideon."

Gideon and Jehoram ran ahead of the rest of the family. Elhanan laughed and shook his head. "Well, that's only natural for two healthy young boys, isn't it?"

There were tears of celebration along with songs of praise and thanksgiving that evening in Elhanan's home. In the near future Rachel and Lucius would need to make plans for their life together. They knew it wouldn't be easy, but most things in life worth anything are not easy. Besides, they knew that God would always be with them if they had faith and asked Him to.

But for now there was only time for praising God and laughing. Elhanan raised his glass of sweet wine. "To Gideon, who had faith in Jesus when everyone was telling him to give up his hope! Thank you, my son, for leading us to Jesus."

THE END

BVG